Her body went slack beneath him, and he knew there was no stopping what he was going to do next.

He kissed her. Beneath the Christmas tree. She tasted like chocolate and spiced rum. That combined with the flavor of her lips made her delicious. It made him greedy, and he couldn't stop himself from going back for more and deepening the kiss. She responded by opening her mouth beneath his and welcoming in his tongue.

He didn't need alcohol tonight. He could happily get drunk off her.

She broke the kiss and set her lips on his jawline, sliding them across and leaving behind little sweet kisses.

He didn't think he had ever been kissed so sweetly in his life. He didn't think he had ever been this turned on in his life, especially by a woman who was wearing so many clothes.

"You're not supposed to be kissing me, Asa Andersen." Her voice was breathy. Sexy. She had no idea how crazy she was driving him. The sweet little schoolteacher made him want to burst out of his skin.

"You're not supposed to be kissing me back."

Dear Reader,

I have always had a deep love for the holiday season…and sexy men in uniform. *Kissed by Christmas* combines those loves into one romance-filled story! You'll travel the country with Asa and Hallie as they meet in snowy New York City and fall in love on the lush Hideaway Island.

I hope you enjoy reading about them as much as I enjoyed writing about them.

xoxo,

Jamie

KISSED by CHRISTMAS

Jamie Pope

HARLEQUIN® KIMANI™ ROMANCE

Recycling programs for this product may not exist in your area.

ISBN-13: 978-0-373-86479-9

Kissed by Christmas

For questions and comments about the quality of this book please contact us at CustomerService@Harlequin.com.

HARLEQUIN®
www.Harlequin.com

Printed in U.S.A.

Jamie Pope first fell in love with romance when her mother placed a novel in her hands at the age of thirteen. She became addicted to love stories and has been writing them ever since. When she's not writing her next book, you can find her shopping for shoes or binge watching shows on Netflix.

Books by Jamie Pope

Harlequin Kimani Romance

Surrender at Sunset
Love and a Latte
A Vow of Seduction (with Nana Malone)
Kissed by Christmas

Visit the Author Profile page
at Harlequin.com for more titles.

To Josh, future driver and manservant.

Chapter 1

Hallie Roberts had never been so cold in her life.

Freezing wasn't accurate.

Bone-cold wasn't enough.

She was arctic-tundra cold. The kind of cold where jumping into a blazing-hot fire wouldn't even be enough to thaw her out.

Her nose was ice. Her toes were so scrunched and frozen in her shoes that they threatened to break off and move back to Florida where they thought they belonged. She didn't blame them—in a few weeks, she was planning to follow.

New York City in December was no joke, especially when it was experiencing a historic cold snap. There was snow on the ground. Mounds and mounds of graying snow and a brutally chilling wind that whipped through her thin but fashionable trench coat and caused her to break out in what seemed like a permanent case of gooseflesh. She hadn't known that weather like this existed. Before she moved from Florida she'd had this romantic idea of winter. Of New York in winter. That it would be all snow-globe beautiful with crystal flakes that gently floated to the ground and made whatever they touched seem magical.

But there was nothing magical about the nor'easter that had covered the city in white. It kept her snowed in and prevented her from going home for Thanksgiving and seeing the family she so sorely missed. So instead of eating her mother's delicious sweet potato pie and slow-cooked ham, and walking on the beach with her grandmother after the big meal, she sat in her apartment and ate General Tso's chicken along with an entire pint of strawberry cheesecake ice cream. And instead of taking an extra day off to breathe in the fresh ocean air and let the sun warm her face, she was trudging through icy snow on her way to work to teach her tenth graders about the brilliance of James Baldwin.

What a way to start the Christmas season.

Even though her plans had been ruined she didn't mind going back to work. Her job was the only thing she liked about New York since she had moved there nearly six months ago. She had been mugged, her brand-new iPhone stolen by a hipster with a full beard wearing an ironic T-shirt. Her car had been towed because she had no idea what alternate-side-of-the-street parking was all about. And she'd once gotten so hopelessly lost on the subway she had to call her cousin back in Florida to help her navigate her way back home because she was too embarrassed to ask for directions. She didn't know anyone in the Big Apple, aside from the people she worked with. She never thought she would be lonely in a city of eight million, but she was. And the longer she stayed here, the more she longed for the sandy beaches and small-town feel of Hideaway Island.

But going back to Hideaway Island wouldn't be easy for her. Back in Hideaway Island was a man who had broken their engagement the day after she had the final fitting for her dress. Back in Hideaway Island was a man who'd told her that he wasn't really sure if he loved her enough to spend the rest of his life with her.

I'm just not sure you're what I need.

I'm not sure if you're good for me at this point in my life.

It was hard being away from her close-knit family for the past half year but it was harder for her living on that tiny island and running into him everywhere she went. They had been together for over five years this time, but they had first started to date in high school. Brent had been her prom date. Nearly every place in town held some sort of special meaning for them. The dock where they had their first kiss. The beach where he proposed to her. The yacht club they were supposed to have their reception in. Reminders of him slapped her in the face at every turn. She had heard about heartbreak, but she had never expected to feel like she had felt.

He had made promises. They had made plans. She had made sacrifices. She had spent the last ten years of her life thinking she was going to be his wife and when he abruptly ended things she knew she would never plan her life around a man again. So when the opportunity came up to teach at this prestigious charter school, she'd jumped on it. Teaching inner-city kids wasn't always easy, but she genuinely enjoyed them.

Except for right that moment when she walked up to the school to see two of her brightest students in the middle of a heated argument.

"You are obviously too stupid to understand what he was saying!"

"Who are you calling stupid? You're the one—"

"Ladies!" Hallie took a step toward them only to feel her foot slide across the sidewalk. It was like the world had slowed down, like she was having an out-of-body experience. Falling down in public was bad enough, but falling in front of a bunch of high schoolers was the stuff nightmares were made of.

Hallie heard someone scream. Maybe it was her. She wasn't sure because she hit the ground hard, her head bouncing on the sidewalk, and then everything went black. She wasn't sure how long she was out or if she had died and gone to heaven, because when she woke up again the most beautiful man in the world was standing over her.

"How was your Thanksgiving, man?" Asa Andersen's partner, Miguel, asked him as they headed back to their station at the end of a long shift.

"Quiet. My sister went to her in-laws' this year so my parents and I went out to a diner."

"A diner!"

"Yeah." Asa grinned. "My father usually does the cooking but he's recovering from the flu and no one wants to eat my mother's food. Trust me, the diner's Thanksgiving special was a thousand times better than anything my mom would have produced."

"Your mom can't cook," Miguel said, moaning as if it were tragic. "I feel for you. You should have come to my house. We have the roasted pork, along with the fried turkey. My grandmother and tías made hundreds of tamales. The pumpkin-pie flan wasn't such a big hit, but my mother's chocolate cake more than made up for it."

"That sounds amazing." Asa couldn't remember the last time they'd had a big holiday meal with aunts and uncles and extended family. Most years it had just been his parents and his sister at the holidays, but since Virginia got married she split her time between her and her husband's family. They saw less of each other now than they ever had and even though he knew that was how things happened, it didn't sit with him too well. It felt like something had been missing.

"My mother sent you a plate," Miguel went on. "And by plate I mean the twelve pounds of food she packed in a huge brown paper bag."

"Your mother is sweet." All of the Gonzaleses were. Sometimes Asa envied his partner. Miguel always had a big, warm family to go to after the end of a long, hard shift.

"My mother wants to hook you up with my little sister but—"

"You stay away from my little sister," Asa finished for him, laughing. "I'm not going anywhere near Arianna, trust me." Arianna was cute, but Asa had been working with Miguel since he joined the FDNY as a rescue paramedic. They were an elite squad of highly trained paramedics that worked alongside the firemen and administered medical care in dangerous, unstable conditions. The last thing he needed was Miguel pissed at him if things didn't work out. Their job was too dangerous for personal feelings to get in the way of the work. "I think you tell everyone to stay away from your little sister. You won't be happy unless she decides to join a convent."

"She'll be married to God. A man can't ask for a better brother-in-law."

"Mine is pretty cool," Asa said as a call came in from dispatch. "I get box seats to any baseball game in the country."

"If you were a legendary shortstop, I would let you date my sister." Miguel picked up the radio. "We're in the area, dispatch. We'll respond." He looked at Asa. "Slip and fall on some black ice. It shouldn't take long."

Asa hit the lights and they drove the two blocks to the scene. Eighty percent of their calls were typical paramedic calls that he rarely thought about when they were done.

It was that other twenty percent that stayed with him. An innocent person getting struck by violence, a car accident that left the vehicle and the people inside of it unrecognizable. Last week Asa had gone through another one of those events that he just couldn't get off his mind.

They had responded to a catastrophic crane collapse last week that had made New York City look like a war zone. Some people didn't make it. Death was an unfortunate part of the job. He should be used to it by now but last week the loss had hit him harder than usual. Maybe it was the time of the year and knowing that a man wouldn't be with his family during the holidays. Maybe it was the fact that he felt that his time with his family was growing shorter and shorter.

The longer he did this job, the more important his family became to him.

They pulled up at the scene in front of Wheatly Academy to see a horde of worried teenagers surrounding a woman on the ground.

"Clear a path, guys," he ordered as they rolled the gurney toward her. "We're here to help her." He took in the woman's appearance and noticed two things. The first was that she definitely wasn't dressed for winter in her brown high-heeled boots and her thin trench coat. The second was that she looked incredibly familiar. But he couldn't place her at the moment. "Does anyone know her name?" he asked the kids.

"She's our English teacher, Miss Roberts," a girl told him. "Hallie is her first name, I think."

"Yeah, it is," a boy confirmed. "We remember it because we say that she's like Halle Berry, but sweeter. Is she going to be okay? She hit her head, really hard."

Asa knelt down to the unconscious woman and touched her cold cheek with the back of his hand. Brain injury was a common effect of a slip and fall. "Hallie?" He called her name and she opened her eyes, looking up at him, and it kind of jolted him. He knew in his gut he had seen this woman before. Seen that beautiful shade of brown skin, seen those large, almond-shaped deep brown eyes with what seemed like a million lashes look up at him.

"Am I dead?" Her voice was soft; there was wonder in it. "Are you an angel? Am I dead?"

"No." He smiled at her. He didn't usually find injured people cute, but this one was exceedingly so. "You slipped on the ice and hit your head. We're going to take you to the hospital to get you checked out."

"Miss, are you okay?" One of the girls asked as she stepped forward.

"No. I'm not." She shut her eyes again. "I remember walking toward you because you and Tiana looked like you were about to engage in World War Three and that's when I slipped." Her voice was much stronger this time. "I blame you two for this fall and that means thirty years of detention for both of you."

"Thirty years!"

"Yup. That's how long I'll be embarrassed about this. I'm not sure I'll survive it."

"But, Miss Roberts! We were just talking about that poem you assigned us last night. I think it's about a boy wanting his mother's approval. Liza thinks it's about romantic love, but clearly she's wrong and takes everything literally because that's how basic she is."

The other girl turned around so quickly Asa was surprised that she didn't have whiplash. "Who are you calling basic?"

"Girls!" Those pretty brown eyes flew open again. "If you don't stop arguing you're both going to be feeling basic when I keep you after school for the next two weeks alphabetizing my book collection by genre. And if you don't think it's that many books, I will gladly go out and get more to keep you busy until prom season."

The girls clamped their mouths shut.

"Well, the good news is that your teacher is lucid, kids," Miguel said stepping forward so that he could stabilize her neck. "The bad news is, she going to be on a war path if you don't give her some space."

"Get to class," she said as her eyes drifted shut briefly, before she opened one of them to survey the crowd. "I'll know if you didn't show up. I'll be checking in, and your papers are still due at the end of the week. You will email them to me."

"Really?" one of the boys asked.

"If you don't believe me, you'll find out what happens if they are late."

The kids scattered. Asa would have, too. Her tone told everyone she wasn't playing. He was surprised that someone who looked so adorable, with her doe eyes and head full of springy black curls, could get a bunch of high schoolers to obey without talking back. His retired military father would have admired that.

"Are they gone?" she asked, looking to Asa again. "My head hurts so much I'm not sure I can see straight."

He nodded. "Ran out of here like they were on fire. Can you tell me what else hurts? Your neck, or back?"

"Just my head." She grabbed his hand and buried it in her hair. "It hurts here."

"That's because you have an epic knot."

"Darn, and I was planning to shave my head this week."

He smiled down at her. "It'll have to wait till after Christmas."

"I don't want them to worry." She looked truly distressed then, and he could see the pain etched into her face. "I have to be tough with them or they'll worry."

"Your students?"

"Yes. They think they are grown, but they are still kids and they'll worry about me. I love them, you know. They are the only reason I stay in this stupid, cold, icy city."

"You're a good teacher," he told her.

"And you're really hot," she said to him. "I like the way your voice sounds. Gentle but strong. Are you sure you're not some sort of jacked angel?"

"He's not," Miguel said. "But he gets that a lot."

Asa shook his head, but he had to admit he was a little flattered. "We're going to take you to the hospital now."

"Okay. Stay with me, Mr. Hot Paramedic."

"I will. I'm not going anywhere."

Chapter 2

The gorgeous man who was sitting by her side as she rode to the hospital had told her that she wasn't dreaming, but she had a hard time believing it. This had to be a dream. They didn't make men who looked like him. Big, beefy, chocolate-colored angels with large hands and beautiful smiles. Or if they did, they weren't walking around like normal people with normal jobs. In fact she was pretty sure she had seen this one on the cover of a fitness magazine. She knew she had seen him before. It was probably the head trauma that made him walk off the pages of a magazine and into her life.

The paramedic was really probably some short, balding middle-aged man with a potbelly, but it didn't matter because he was so lovely. He made busting her behind in public kind of nice.

"You still with me, Hallie?" he asked in his deep, soothing voice as he touched her hand.

"I am. What's your name? I'm feeling a little loopy. Did I ask you that already? I'm not sure what I've been saying."

"You didn't ask. My name is Asa. Do you know where you are going?"

Hallie gasped. "Healer." Now she knew she must be hallucinating. "I'm with a healer on my way to the hospital."

He looked truly surprised. "You know the meaning of my name?"

She nodded but it hurt her head and she shut her eyes. "Your name is healer and you have the body of a god. It's perfect. Truly perfect. Did you pick your career based on your name?"

"No, ma'am," he said, and she could hear the smile in his voice. "I was supposed to be a doctor. I made it all the way through medical school and quit in my intern year."

"Oh, that must have killed your mother."

He laughed. "It did. I think she's still in mourning. But she forgot about me when my twin sister became a painter."

"A painter. Code for starving artist. What was she supposed to be?"

"A college professor, but she ended up being an interior designer."

"That's funny. My dream was to get my doctorate and become a college professor. It's not for everyone. Is your sister happy?"

"She's very happy."

"Oh, I love to hear that. You're happy too, right? That's all that matters. That you're happy. Happiness is the most important thing on the planet." Hallie wasn't sure why she couldn't stop talking or what was making her say the things she was saying, but she couldn't stop herself. This man was a stranger. He probably thought she was insane and maybe she was, but there was just something about him that made her comfortable.

His name had been well chosen. Just his calm manner soothed her. She should have been scared out of her mind, going to the hospital in a city she still didn't know well, about missing work, and not having proper sub plans, but none of that mattered to her at the moment.

"I like my job very much."

"But are you happy, Asa?"

He was quiet for a long as he looked down at her. "We're here," he told her. "They are probably going to do some neurological tests and a CAT scan. Give you something for the pain if you need it. You remember where you live, right?"

She opened her eyes and looked at him. He was still the same beautiful man that had been there since she had first opened her eyes. "In a fifth floor walkup in the Village that is smaller than my childhood bedroom."

"Oh." He nodded, a strange expression on his face. "Is there anyone for you to call?"

"No. I'm here all by myself. My family is South."

"What about friends from work? Can you call someone to get you home?"

"I can call a cab."

He looked hesitant and for the first time since she had hit her head, Hallie started to worry. "Is something wrong? Do you think I won't be able to get home without help?"

He shook his head. "I'm sure you will. I just don't like the idea of leaving you here all alone."

"I have to get used to being alone. I'll be okay," she said as the door opened. "Thank you."

"For what?" he asked as they rolled her out.

"For being kind to me."

"I wasn't. I was just doing my job."

"You're very good at it. Thank you for that."

"What the hell was that?" Miguel asked him as they drove away fifteen minutes later.

"What?" Asa asked, still distracted by the woman they had just left behind.

"I'm used to women mooning over you. It makes me feel like I look like dog food, but it is what it is. This time I sensed something weird going on between you two. Granted, the lady was out of it from knocking her head, but you were weird, too."

"I'm not weird. She lives in my building. She's three doors down from me."

"And she didn't recognize you?"

"I haven't lived there for that long. Just a few months and you know we work crazy hours. I couldn't place her at first but I knew I knew her from somewhere and it was bugging me."

"And you think she's cute."

"She is cute," he admitted. She was more than cute. He found himself truly attracted to a patient, which had never happened to him. "A lot of women in New York are cute."

"I like the way she handled those kids. She said go and they scattered like roaches."

He nodded, smiling at the memory. "She made me think of my sister. I'm glad she's married now. Before, she moved all around the world alone. Anything could have happened to her. But Hallie said she was all alone in the city. If she'd landed the wrong way or just hit her head a little harder, it would have been another story and her family wouldn't even be near her."

"This kind of stuff never bothered you before. You've been a little bit off since the crane collapse."

"And you haven't?" He had taken this job because he loved the excitement, the rush he got when the lights and sirens were going, knowing that he was going to use his skills to save lives. And this one had started out that way, but when they got there it had turned out different. It had been one of the worst scenes he had ever been to. He had been on the scene for fires, helped rescue a man out of an iced-over river, but it looked like a bomb had gone off in the middle of New York City. Dust and debris and pandemonium everywhere. Ten people injured, one died on the scene from massive chest injuries and the other man had died at the hospital later from a heart attack.

"I try not to think about." Miguel shrugged. "The nature of a job. There might be something worse just around the corner."

Asa had thought about those words all the way home that day. Hallie had asked him if he was happy. He had never thought about it before. He loved his job. He was having fun in New York dating some interesting women. But was he happy? Lately he had been feeling like something was missing in his life. Maybe Miguel was right, maybe the crane collapse had just put him in a weird head space.

He went home, made himself something to eat and tried to get some rest. He should be exhausted after working back-to-back shifts, but his mind kept going back to Hallie, wondering how she was. If she'd gotten home okay. Part of him wondered if he would have put her out of his mind had he not known she was his neighbor, but a bigger part of him thought that she was just the kind of person that would stay with him.

He got up and left his apartment. It would be easy enough to check. Then he could just go back to his life.

He knocked on her door, listening for sounds inside. If she wasn't home he could check with the hospital. Most of the time they never knew what happened to the people they transported, but Asa could find out, see if she needed help. Perhaps contact a family member for her. It was what he would have wanted someone to do for his sister.

He knocked again and this time he heard rustling from

inside of the apartment. He waited for a moment and then she opened the door. She wore sweats and fuzzy pink socks on her feet. Her springy curls stood out in every direction. Her eyes widened when she saw him and a guarded look crossed her face immediately.

"What are you doing here?" It certainly wasn't the same greeting he had gotten when he'd first approached her that day.

"I came to see if you got home okay."

"I did. How do you know where I live? Did you follow me home? I may have hit my head, but if you think you can abuse your position and try to take advantage of me, you have another think coming."

"Whoa." Asa put his hands up in defense. "Why the hell would you think I would try to take advantage of you?"

"You showed up at my door. You knew I lived alone. How many women have you followed home before? I bet they let you in because you're charming and good-looking. But it's not happening this time. I should call and report you to your supervisor."

Asa felt his anger rising, but he tried to tamp it down. What was she supposed to think? It must have been scary for her to see a strange man show up at her door. "I'm your neighbor. I live at the end of the hall in 4D. I sure as hell didn't follow you home. We bumped into each other once when I was moving in. I've seen you at the mailboxes before."

She paused for a moment and he could see the pain and sleepiness on her face. "Prove it to me."

"You want to see my lease?"

"That would be nice, but just show me that you can get into your apartment."

"Okay." For a moment he wanted to refuse, but the last

thing he needed was for the little schoolteacher calling up the FDNY and complaining that he was stalking her.

He took a step back and she came out of her apartment with a metal baseball bat.

"You always answer the door with that?"

"When I'm not expecting visitors. My mother got it for me when she heard I moved here."

"Smart." He had to give her that. She should bash the head in of any man who tried to mess with her. He stopped in front of his door and pushed it open to reveal his large studio apartment.

"It's twice the size of my place!" She stepped inside, her mouth agape, and even though he was annoyed with her he had to admit that she was still mighty cute.

"Here's some of my mail. Addressed to me here." He thrust some envelopes at her. "And here is a picture of me with my parents when I completed my training with the FDNY." He pointed to the framed black-and-white photo on the wall.

"Oh." She placed his mail back on the little side table he had taken it from. "I'm sorry. You do live here. You're the guy who had all the big, hot guys move him in. You apologized to me for the noise the day you moved in. I can't believe I didn't recognize you."

"You hit your head and I keep irregular hours. It took me a little while to place you, too."

She placed a hand on her forehead as if she were in pain. "What did I say to you today? Was it crazy? I know I was out of it, but was it as crazy as I think it was?"

"No." He started feeling the need to tease her a bit. "It was just something about me being an angel with a perfect body."

"Oh, no." She groaned deeply and walked toward the door. "I'm going to crawl under my bed and die now."

"Hey!" He grabbed her arm and turned her around. "I know you were joking, but don't joke like that, especially after a head injury. What did the hospital say?"

"That I'm not allowed to go to work and that I need to rest for the next few days because I might have some lingering pain and dizziness. But I'll be fine. I'm going to go in."

"No, you're not." He cupped her face in his hands and looked into her large almond eyes. "Your eyes are watery. I can tell that you're still in pain. You're not going to work tomorrow. You're going to follow the doctor's orders and rest."

"How exactly are you going to stop me?" She looked up at him defiantly.

"I liked you a lot better when you were dazed from a blow to the head."

"Listen, I just spent the last five days alone in my apartment due to this stupid freak snowstorm we had. The last thing I want is to spend another week alone in my apartment. Those kids are the only reason I'm still living here. I don't want to miss a week of work."

She was dedicated to her students, and maybe she was lonely being all alone in this big city, but he couldn't allow her to risk her health.

"I'll come by tomorrow." He hadn't meant to say it, but it slipped out and he couldn't take it back. He felt the need to look after her. Like there was a reason that he and Miguel, out of all the EMTs and paramedics, had responded to the call when they were technically off duty. "Just to check on you, and just in case you get any ideas it's not to stalk you or take advantage of you, or any other twisted thing you thought up."

She nodded and it was then he realized he still had her face in his hands. Her face was so small in his hands and her skin was so smooth. He resisted the urge to run his thumbs across her cheeks. He removed his hands from her face and stepped away from her.

"Get some rest, Hallie."

"I will. Good night, Asa."

She left then and Asa was sure that he was going to be seeing a lot more of his neighbor.

Chapter 3

Hallie could barely move the next morning. She had really thought about defying Asa and going to work anyway, sure she would be feeling a hundred percent better when she woke up, but that wasn't the case. She felt like she had been hit by a large truck that had backed up and run over her again. The noise from the television hurt her ears. Looking at a computer screen caused a sharp pain to go right through her head, so she just lay in bed and reached for her cell phone.

Her cousin was on speed dial. She missed her family painfully, but it was her cousin whom she had the hardest time being away from. Derek was the mayor of their small town of Hideaway Island. He had encouraged her to move on after her breakup with Brent. He had given her the courage to step away from everything she had known and live a life that was simply just for her and no one else. But while she was living just for herself, she found herself missing the slow-paced life of her island home and the people that made living there so wonderful.

Her head throbbed steadily as she placed the phone to her ear, and she wanted to curse her cousin. If it weren't for his unfailing support, she would have never slipped on the ice in the first place.

"My favorite cousin!" his deep voice boomed through the phone.

"Bite me," she replied.

"Whoa. I'm pretty sure your mother taught you that you aren't supposed to greet people like that."

"I have a concussion. Spent all day in the hospital after I slipped on the ice heading to work and hit my head in front of a bunch of teenagers, and it's all your fault. You big dumb jerk."

"Did I cause you to fall?" he asked seriously. "I don't remember flying to New York and giving you a shove. But if I did, I apologize."

"You made me move to a terribly cold place."

"I didn't. I encouraged you to get off the island and be away from that pretentious jackass who you were giving up your dreams for. You took the job in New York because it was a great opportunity. I happen to like New York. It's a great city. I would live there if my heart wasn't so connected to this place."

"I miss home." She sighed. "I miss you, too."

"You must have really hurt your head if you are admitting to missing me. Are you okay?"

"I'm fine," she said, but could hear the weariness in her own voice.

"I'm serious. Are you really okay? I can catch a flight out of Miami this afternoon and be there tonight."

"No." He was protective of her. The big brother she needed. "You don't have to. I was just calling to ask you to look for flights for me. I have a long winter break this year and really need to be home for Christmas. I would look myself but I'm not supposed to be on the computer."

"Does your mother know that you got hurt?" The worry in his voice was clear.

"Of course not. She would have heart failure if she did."

"She worried all Thanksgiving about you. She was sure you were going to starve that day because nothing would be open for the holiday."

"That's one thing I love about New York. There's always something open." She suddenly got extremely tired, almost letting the phone slip out of her hand.

"Hallie? Hallie!"

"I'm here. I just zoned out for a moment," she said as she heard the knock on her door. She already suspected she knew who was standing on the other side of the door.

"I really think I should come up there. You don't sound like yourself."

"I'm fine. My neighbor is here to check on me. He went to med school."

"But you didn't say he's a doctor."

"He's not." She eased herself out of bed, feeling every one of her muscles protest. "He's a paramedic. I've got to go, Derek. He'll probably break down the door if I don't open."

"Who is this guy? I've never heard you mention him before."

"That's because I didn't know him before. Please let me know about the flights."

She disconnected before he had the chance to question her any more. The phone call seemed to zap the tiny bit of energy she did have out of her.

The knocking on her door had turned to full banging by the time she got there. Asa stood there, his beautiful face twisted with concern. It wasn't fair that he got to walk around looking like that. He wasn't dressed for work today. She had expected he would be and on the way to a shift but he was in jeans and a T-shirt. Looking just as good in that as he did in his dark blue uniform.

"You look like hell." He stepped inside, took her face in his hands and looked into her eyes. Normally she would slap any man who touched her face like that after knowing her for twenty-four hours but she didn't mind Asa's hands on her skin. Big, warm hands that were a combination of rough and smooth and felt soothing when nothing else did.

"Gee, thanks."

"You're in pain."

She attempted to nod, but couldn't bring herself to do it. "Yes."

"Just your head?"

"No. All over."

"A side effect from slipping on ice. You probably have some minor soft tissue damage."

He took a penlight out of his pocket and shined it in her eyes, which caused her to wince.

"Pupils look fine, but you have some light sensitivity. Sound, too?"

"Yes."

"Turn around," he murmured. He slipped his hand beneath her shirt and ran his fingers along her spine. It was in a medical way, not an ounce of seduction there, but Hallie had to admit that she liked the sensation of his hands on her bare skin. It had been a very long time since a man had touched her at all. Even when she was with Brent, their lovemaking had been very scheduled, very ordinary, pleasant but almost mechanical. Hallie was feeling different with Asa than she did with Brent and all he was doing was checking to see if she was injured. She wanted to chalk it up to being celibate for so long, and figured that she might react this way with any good-looking man but she knew it had more to do with Asa being Asa.

"No sore or tender spots?" he asked as he continued his examination. "Bend over for me just a little like you're going to touch your feet."

She did as he asked as his hands traveled across her back. "Does anything hurt when you do that? Any particular pain or twinge?"

"I'm just sore all over. My tailbone hurts the most."

He pulled the band of her pants just a bit and looked. "You've got a bit of a bruise there." He straightened her to standing and turned her around to face him where his fingers slid to the back of the neck.

"How's your neck?"

"Stiff," she answered and as soon as the word came out of her mouth his touch stopped being medical. He rubbed her aching muscles with his thick, long fingers. Too sore and sleepy to think about what she was doing, she pushed herself against him while he did it.

Asa's intentions were pure when he'd begun his examination of Hallie. She'd opened the door and her appearance had knocked him in the gut. He could tell that she was in pain, her big beautiful eyes dull, her skin tone ashen. He still found her beautiful, but more than that he had this overwhelming need to take care of her. It was something he had never felt before, like something internal that was pushing him to. And then when he was examining her lower back, his need to take care of her had changed into a different kind of need all caused by the little tattoo of a seahorse on her back.

He had been surprised to see it there and then he realized what he had been doing, running his hands all along this woman's body. Slightly aroused by her when he knew he shouldn't be. He turned her around to face him, knowing he should stop, that he should go home, knowing that he had done his duty. But he looked at her tired, sad face again and couldn't step away from her. She was a stranger, but he felt like he knew her, like he was supposed to be there. It was a crazy thought, but as he went to rub her neck and she pushed her soft body against his he knew that maybe he wasn't the only one who felt a connection.

"Don't think I'm crazy," she said softly as she wrapped her arms around him. "But I think I'm going to cry."

"It's okay." He stroked his hand down her back. "I know you're in pain."

"It's not that. You smell good and your body is so warm and I miss my family. It's been a long time since I've been hugged."

"It must have been hard to be away from your family on the holiday."

His parents were a few hours away in New Jersey so it hadn't been that long since he had been hugged, but he couldn't think of the last time he'd had a beautiful woman wrapped around him. He dated, frequently. He enjoyed women, but lately it had just been dates. He hadn't invited anyone back to his place. He hadn't spent the night at anyone else's. He could have, but ever since his twin had gotten married he'd felt off. Odd. Like there was something missing in his life. Virginia was so happy. The women that Asa dated didn't make him happy. They were just someone to pass the time with.

It was strange to be having those kinds of thoughts while he was holding a woman he barely knew, but he couldn't stop them.

"I'm fine now." She pulled away from him and he found himself missing her warmth. He should just go back home and forget about her. His mind could be soothed now. She was a little banged up, but he was sure she would be fine.

"You should take a hot bath with Epsom salts. It will make you feel better."

"That sounds amazing." She moaned a little and it made him harden just a bit. "But there's a problem."

"What?"

"I don't have either of those things."

"You don't have a bathtub?"

"Have you seen the size of this place?"

He looked around him. He really hadn't paid attention to it before, but it was tiny. Just one long room. He could see the entirety of it from where he stood. But it was cozy. It looked like her. She had a white gauzy curtain around her bed, which was made with a fluffy white-and-black floral-printed comforter. There was a small love seat beside it and a vintage wood desk that had been painted a soft blue. Besides the old fireplace that Asa was sure was no longer functional, there was nothing else to the space. They were standing in her kitchen. He turned around to see that her bathroom only had a shower.

"I have a tub."

"My place could fit inside of your place three times. How can you afford it? Do paramedics make that much?" She looked pained then. "That's one of those questions I'm not supposed to ask."

"I happened to be there when the owner of the building was hit by a livery cab. I stabilized him until the paramedics arrived on scene."

"You saved his life," she said softly.

"No. I did what I was supposed to do. But he was grateful and he tracked me down to thank me. When he found out where I was living he told me his son was moving out of this building and offered the apartment to me at the same price his son was paying."

"Oh. Did you follow him home to check on him, too?"

He grinned at her. "No. But I did visit him in the hospital."

"Are you sure you're a real person? No one cares that much."

"I have a family. If it were my father, I would have wanted somebody who went through medical training to be there with him until help arrived. And you made me think about my sister. I wouldn't want her hurt and alone in a strange city."

"I'm not sure that I could ever be that good of a person."

"I'm sure you're wrong." They looked at each other for a long moment, the urge to pull her closer and wrap his arms back around her growing stronger.

"I hate you a little," she said changing the subject. "You mentioned the word *bath* and now it's all I can think of."

"You can take one at my place. My tub is pretty big."

Her eyes widened. "With you?"

"Alone. Unless you really want me there. I thought we made it clear that I wasn't going to try anything. I try to stay away from women with fresh head injuries. You don't have to take me up on my offer."

"But I will." She turned away from him and grabbed a robe out of her closet and some fresh pajamas. He knew that this wasn't the typical favor that one neighbor did for another but he couldn't take back the offer. He wasn't ready to leave her alone just yet and knew his instincts were right when he saw how slowly she moved, like her body was stiff with pain.

A few minutes later they were in his bathroom, which by New York City standards was huge, with a deep tub and a wall with tiles that had been salvaged from old buildings. The shower was separate from the tub and was enclosed in glass.

It was a million times better than his last place and as

he sat down on the side of the tub to turn on the water, he knew it would take an act of God to get him to move out of this place.

"I can definitely tell that a man lives here, but this bathroom looks like it has been designed by a woman."

"It might have been. The guy who lived here before me moved out because his fiancée left him. He moved to LA."

"Oh, I know that story."

"Do you?"

"Why do you think I came to New York?" She gave him a small smile. "My fiancé called off our wedding just before I was supposed to walk down the aisle. He wasn't sure if I was the kind of wife he wanted, or if he loved me enough to spend forever with me."

"Stupid bastard." He got up, brushing past her to grab the Epsom salts and lightly scented oil and bubble bath he kept under the sink.

"Why do you think he's the stupid one? It could be me. You don't know."

He looked at her for a long moment. "I know." Any man who broke up with a woman like that after he asked her to marry him was cruel.

She gave him another soft smile. There was a sweetness about her and he wanted to pull her mouth to his just to see if he could taste it.

"You look like a man who has run a lot of baths for women," she said as he added everything to the hot water.

"I've been known to take a bath from time to time. I was a college football player. I took a lot of hits and last year I did a Spartan Sprint and dislocated my elbow. The hot water usually soothes it when it starts acting up"

"A Spartan Sprint? Is that one of those 5K mud runs?"

He shook his head. "My brother-in-law and I did a long-distance one. Twenty-seven obstacles. There was fire, mud and barbed wire. We would have been the fastest team if I hadn't slipped."

"That sounds like my worst nightmare."

"We're going to do another one in Miami in March."

"Crazy. I can barely walk down the street without falling and you sign up for death runs."

"You sound like my mother."

They grinned at each other for a moment before he looked back at his tub that seemed inviting. He had never taken a bath with a woman. He liked his private time, but it was something he might like to try with her.

"I'll leave you alone now. Take as long as you want in here."

"Thank you, Asa."

He nodded and left her.

He settled in to read, but he couldn't concentrate on the words because his thoughts kept returning to the presumably naked woman in his bathroom.

A knock on his door saved him from trying to go back to his book. He found his mother standing there. She was looking fashionably proper, with her hair swept up elegantly and wearing a gray wool coat that would probably never go out of style. Dr. Andersen might have a PhD in advanced mathematics, but she was no absentminded academic. She could intimidate nearly anyone she came across and that was why Asa was uneasy about her unexpected appearance at his door. It had nothing to do with the woman in his bathtub.

"Mom? Hey. What are you doing here?"

She breezed past him with a smile on her face. "Do I need an excuse to see my baby boy?"

"Um. No? You just never drop by unannounced."

"I was in the city to have lunch with a former colleague at Columbia and I thought I would stop by. I have something to tell you and I figured I should do it in person rather than over the phone."

He sat down hard on the stool at his breakfast bar. "Are you sick?"

"No! Of course not."

"Are you divorcing Dad?"

"Asa! Do you think I would look this happy if I were divorcing your father or sick?"

"I don't know, Mom. You could be coming over here to tell me that you're running away to Bora Bora with one of your students."

"I'm not sure where you got such an imagination from. You're starting to sound like your sister."

"Did you tell her the news?"

"She knows. It was her idea."

"It was Gin's idea and you're happy about it?" He crossed his arms across his chest. "This I've got to hear."

"Your sister wants to throw a big get-together at her house on Hideaway Island with both families. It's going to be wonderful—two weeks of holiday festivities, topped off with a huge Christmas party they are inviting the whole island to. I'm so excited. And I'm making the point of telling you that you're going to use up that vacation time you have accrued and spend the whole time with us down there."

"Okay," he agreed.

"No argument? No, 'I have plans,' or 'a date?' Or something more important than following your mother's dreams and wishes?"

"I was planning to see Virginia at Christmas anyway. You could have told me this over the phone. What else is going on?"

"Your father and I are retiring to Florida. I put in my paperwork yesterday and we've officially put the house on the market. We are going to be looking at homes on Hideaway Island while we're there."

"Oh." He wasn't expecting her to say that. He had always pictured his parents living in their Cape Cod–style home, but it made sense for them to move. His father had hurt his back shoveling the heavy snow more than once. And he had been retired from the military for years now. None of their children were home. There was no reason for them to stay. They should go but he felt odd about it. "Congratulations, Mom. The school will miss you."

"Is there something wrong, sweetheart?" She touched his cheek and in that same moment he heard his bathroom door open. Out stepped Hallie in a short blush-colored robe. Her curly hair was damp, but he could see her perfect ringlets forming. Her eyes went wide when she saw his mother there, and he found Hallie to be incredibly beautiful.

"Well, who do we have here?" his mother asked.

"Hallie, this is my mother, Dr. Andersen. Mom, this is Hallie. She lives in 4A." He could have explained why Hallie was there, but he didn't want to. He was thirty-two years old and if he wanted to have a woman in his apartment, he would have a woman in his apartment.

"It's nice to meet you, ma'am." Hallie started to rush forward, hand extended, but then stopped. He could see the pain on her face.

Asa went to her, his hand impulsively reaching out to touch her cheek. "Are you okay?"

"Yes. I almost forgot that my body is one big, giant sack of soreness."

"Did the bath help?"

"A lot. Thank you."

"How's your head?"

"I'll take some aspirin when I get home. I'll be fine."

"Are you okay, dear?" His mother stepped forward. There was genuine concern on her face.

"I'm fine. I just fell on the ice yesterday and gave myself a little concussion. Your son came to my rescue. I was coming to tell you it was nice to meet you and then get out of your hair. I didn't mean to interfere with your plans. You have a very nice son, Dr. Andersen."

"Thank you, Hallie." His mother looked at him and gave him a smile. "He's a good man."

"I'll see you around, Asa. Thank you again."

He grabbed her hand, stopping her from fleeing. "You don't have to leave. You're not interfering with anything."

"We didn't have plans," his mother added. "I was just stopping by. You shouldn't be alone when you have a concussion. Sit down on the couch and I'll make you some tea. Have you eaten anything today?"

"No ma'am, but—"

"No buts. You take yourself over to the couch this moment. Asa, help me find the tea and use that app on your phone to order us something for lunch. Italian, I think. Or maybe deli. What do you think, Hallie?"

"Whatever you want, Dr. Andersen."

"I think you need pasta and bread. It's settled. Go sit down now and I'll bring you your tea."

"Yes, ma'am." Hallie did as she was told, leaving Asa and his mother heading to his kitchen.

"That girl is just darling. I like her already. A much different direction than your usual conquest. What's her story?"

"She's not one of my conquests. She's my neighbor. She's a high school teacher at Wheatly Academy."

His mother gave an approving nod. "I've heard great things about Wheatly. They take brilliant but at-risk youth and prepare them for college. They only hire the most qualified teachers. Your girlfriend must be bright."

"She is bright. Her dream is to become a college professor, but she's not my girlfriend."

"A college professor! Why didn't you tell me about her sooner?" She rummaged through his cabinet for the tea he kept there just for her.

"There's nothing to tell. I barely know her."

She slanted a brow at him. "I saw the way you looked at her. Sweet, pretty, educated. She's perfect for you. Maybe I'll finally get some grandchildren. Your sister has been married for nearly two years and stubbornly refuses to give me one. Maybe if she knows she's in competition with you it will speed her up."

"She's enjoying traveling with her husband. Carlos just retired from baseball at the end of the season."

"You've both done enough traveling." She touched his face. "Don't ruin this for me, Asa. I might never like another one of your girlfriends again."

Chapter 4

Hallie snuggled into the warm, hard surface she was sleeping on. She had slept on softer mattresses but she liked the feeling of this one. She had been so cold since she had been in New York, like a chill had seeped to her bones and never let up. But tonight it was finally gone and for once she felt warm and protected. It was when she felt a hand gently rest on her cheek that she realized that her warm, hard mattress was a warm, hard body.

She remembered where she was and she knew that she should move, but she didn't want to. She didn't want to lose this feeling that she was sure she would never have again while she was here, but she lifted her head and looked up at Asa. "I can't believe you let me fall asleep on you."

"You needed to sleep. You injured your brain. It needs rest to recover."

She was feeling a little better despite the stiffness in her body. The Andersens had really taken care of her today. Dr. Andersen had bossed her around, ordered her to put her feet up and eat more and drink extra fluids. It was heavenly. She hadn't been mothered in a long time. It was nice to experience it, even if it came from someone else's mother. "Where is your mother? She must think I'm awful."

"She went home about two hours ago."

"Two hours ago! How long have I been out?"

"You went down about a half hour before she left."

"You let me sleep on you that long?"

"It started out with just your head on my shoulder, but you curled up like that a half hour ago or so."

"You should have woken me."

"I didn't see a reason to."

"What did your mother say about me? 'Where on earth did you find that dizzy girl? And do you always let women you barely know use your bathroom?'" She could only imagine what the beautiful, proper professor thought about the strange woman with the head injury who had somehow gotten involved with her son. "I can't imagine a worse first impression to make."

"She likes you."

"She was being polite."

Asa shook his head. "Trust me, Hallie. If my mother didn't like you she would make it known. My mother may have excellent manners, but she has no problem stating her opinion. She had my last girlfriend in tears their first meeting."

"Oh. I can see that. She scares me a little. Why didn't she like your last girlfriend?"

"She called herself Bambi and when she met my mother she was wearing a top that was so low-cut you could see… All the gifts God gave her. Plus she wore jeans that were cut so low you could see her thong."

"I think your mother should have made *you* cry. Why would you bring home a woman like that when you knew your parents would be disapproving? It's like you set that poor lady up."

"I didn't. My parents were in the city and asked if they could take us to lunch. I wasn't planning on introducing them that day. Bambi was dressed like that when I picked her up and I didn't feel like it was my place to ask or tell her to wear something that would please my mother. Would you want a man telling you how to dress?"

He had a point. "No. My ex was like that. I was supposed to dress a certain way. Speak a certain way. Behave a certain way. All to keep up with the image he had crafted. I hated it."

"What's wrong with the way you speak, dress and behave?"

"I just wasn't right. My ex-fiancé is a Realtor who specializes in luxury properties. It was a small family business that he had grown over the years. He wanted to cater to the wealthy jet-set crowd and celebrities and I was supposed to be.... I'm not sure who or what he wanted me to be, but in the end I couldn't deliver."

"Thank God for that. You shouldn't be with a man who doesn't think you're good enough."

"I knew it was going to end when he asked me to straighten my hair. I had worn it straight sometimes, but he asked me to wear it straight whenever I accompanied him somewhere special. I told him no. He barely spoke to me for three days. When we broke up, I cut it short and haven't seen a flatiron since."

"I like your curls. They're beautiful." He lifted his hand to her hair and sunk his fingers deep inside her ringlets. It was not something she normally let anyone do. But she didn't mind him doing it. She liked his soothing touch and the way his fingers felt as they gently scratched her scalp.

She closed her eyes again. This was how she had fallen asleep before. He lulled her with his deep voice and calming conversation. She was comfortable around him. "Tell me more about Bambi."

"There's not much to tell. She was a cocktail waitress. Fun, sweet. Someone that was easy to hang out with but not someone you would discuss anything deep with. She was exactly what I was looking for at the time."

"How did your mother make her cry?"

"She asked her a question," he said evasively.

"Are you going to tell me what it was?"

"I don't think my mother meant it the way it sounded. She's an academic. She's from a very conservative family. Her only option in life was to use her brain."

"You don't have to explain your mother to me, Asa. I can tell that she's a good person."

He nodded. "She asked Bambi what her future plans were. She wanted to know what she was going to do when her body stopped being in that kind of shape and she could no longer use her sexuality to get good tips. And then she said something about sagging skin and breasts and that's the first time I had ever wished for a huge natural disaster."

"You could have used a big meteor striking the restaurant."

"I think Bambi said something about getting married and raising a family. I'll never forget what my mother said then. 'Being a wife and mother are wonderful things, but haven't you ever considered that you have more to offer the world? Haven't you ever thought about how you were going to leave your mark?' Bambi burst into tears then. We broke up after that."

"She never wanted to see you again after that meeting?"

"No. She was looking to get serious and I knew there was no point. I want to be with someone who has more to offer the world than their body. I hate it when my mother is right."

Hallie smiled and leaned in to kiss Asa. As soon as she felt her mouth press against his, she realized what she had just done. It was just a simple kiss, just two sets of lips pressing against each other, but as she did it she knew she had felt more kissing him than she had felt kissing Brent for the last five years.

There was nothing sexual, nothing hot or explosive between them, but she felt a lovely warmth spread throughout her entire body and a very sturdy tug on her heart. Almost like it had been kicked awake.

"Oh." She pulled away from him. "I didn't mean to do that. I shouldn't have done that."

"No. You shouldn't have," he said just before he tumbled her backward on the couch and kissed her again.

She knew that they shouldn't be doing this, but his heavy body settled on top of hers and it felt right. His kiss was deeper. More sensuous. It was open mouths and tongues sweeping across each other. It was slow and shocking. She knew it was too much for her senses and yet she wanted so much more. She knew without a doubt that this was the best kiss of her life and then he broke it. She lay there with her chest heaving and her eyes closed. It was a beautiful moment.

"I'm not stopping because I want to, but because I know we shouldn't go any further."

She opened her eyes and looked up into his handsome face. "I know." She let out a long sigh.

"I've wanted to kiss you all day. I wanted to be in the bathtub with you and run a washcloth over your naked back. I wanted to pull you close and keep you there more times than I could count today."

Hallie felt another painful tug in her heart again. Why was this happening now? Why did it have to be him who responded to the call yesterday? She was still heartsore from her broken engagement. The last thing she needed was a romantic entanglement, especially if she wasn't sure if she was going to last much longer in this city. "Asa. Don't say that to me."

"Why? It's true. I won't lie to you."

"I don't need sex right now, but I do need a friend." She surprised herself by saying so. It would be easy for her to go back to her apartment. For her to ignore him, forget about this day and all he had done for her. But she knew that would be too hard. It wouldn't be easy to just be his friend, but she knew she'd rather have him in her life like that, than to go back to being completely alone in this big scary place. "Can you be my friend?"

He sat up, pausing for a moment, before he nodded. "I can."

"Good. You can start by walking me home."

Asa got up and walked Hallie down the hall. He could still feel her lips on his, could still feel how her body went pliant beneath his. He could taste the sweetened tea on her lips and when she'd returned his kiss by sweeping her tongue into his mouth he'd felt jolted, a rush that he couldn't put into words.

She'd curled his fingers into his shirt. She had wrapped her leg around him. She'd let out a little moan when he broke the kiss. He had wanted to kiss her all day—he just hadn't expected it to be an experience.

He'd stopped because he was growing too aroused, far too quickly. She was still suffering from a concussion and as much as he wanted her he knew that he couldn't take things any further that night.

And then she'd asked him to be her friend. It was like someone had thrown cold water on him. She had every right to ask him that. He could see things going too quickly with her. The kind of attraction he had for her was dangerous. He barely knew her, but he knew she wasn't the kind of woman to jump into bed with a man. She was alone in this city and still recovering from a bad breakup.

It would be foolish to jump into something with him.

They stopped in front of her door and he watched her as she opened it and stepped inside. She turned to face him. "Good night, Asa."

"Good night."

"And thank you." She reached to hug him, pressing that sweet, curvy body against his once again. "For everything."

He wrapped his arms around her and hugged her back, holding her tightly against him. He *would* be her friend, but he knew he would kiss her again, too. He wouldn't be able not to. There was no way to prevent it if she was anywhere near him.

There was a knock at Hallie's door just before 6:00 p.m. that next evening. It was her second day off work and she was feeling only slightly better. Her body was still stiff and sore, although the constant heavy throbbing in her head had lessened and her dizziness had mostly subsided. She'd thought she was nearly back to normal when she left Asa's last night and that she would be ready to go back to work again. The pain had been completely gone when she woke up on his chest last evening. There was no dizziness at all, maybe just some headiness. His kiss had kept her floating all night. It had her thinking of him and his soft, firm lips when she went to bed. It had her dreaming of him on top of her, beside her, his hands roaming all over her, his breath tickling her skin. But she hadn't slept as well in her bed as she had when she was curled up against him. It had been one time, for a few hours, but as she lay in her bed alone, she felt like something was missing, like he was missing.

Her heart sped up as she walked to the door. It was probably him, coming to see how she was.

She opened the door to find a woman there. She was short, Hispanic, very pretty with long black hair that had a dramatic gray stripe running down the center of it. She was dressed in some kind of a uniform and holding two large paper bags. "Ms. Roberts?" There was a touch of an accent in her voice.

"Yes."

"My name is Rosa Nieves. I'm Charlie's mother."

"Oh, hello. It's nice to meet you. I spoke with your husband during conference week."

"Yes. Charlie told me that you had fallen in front of the school and hit your head. He's been worried. All the kids are worried about you."

"They're sweet. The doctor wants me to stay home for at least a week. Hopefully, I'll be cleared to go back to work by Monday."

"We hope so, too. My son never used to tell me anything, but he told me about you and I figured you must be special. He likes your class. He told me you taught him about the Nuyorican movement and he's become very interested in that playwright Miguel Piñero. He's talking about going to college to study writing. He's never talked about going to college before. I don't know how we'll pay for it, but we'll find a way."

"Charlie is incredibly bright. I have a list of scholarships that he's eligible for. We'll figure it out. He'll have the life you hoped he would."

"Thank you. That's why I'm here. To thank you. The school gave me your address so I could deliver this. I work around the corner in an office building and I swear I'll never come back here to bother you. But I wanted to do this. Me and a couple of parents from the school made you enough food to last you a week. Some of the dishes are still hot. I made you coquito cupcakes and there is some breakfast stuff, as well as some lunch meat. Some of the kids wrote you letters, too."

"Oh." Hallie was breathless. Her vision had gone blurry. "This was so kind of you. Thank you. That doesn't feel like a big enough word but I really don't know what else to say."

"Don't cry, honey. Just get better and get back to school. Those kids need you." She placed the bags on the floor inside the door, just as Asa walked up. He was wearing his uniform.

"What's the matter? Why are you crying, Hallie?"

"The parents at my school are very kind. Thank you, Mrs. Nieves."

"You're welcome. Just get some rest. I'm glad you have someone here to take care of you."

"But..."

Mrs. Nieves walked away before Hallie could clarify things. Asa was standing there, looking extremely handsome and slightly concerned. "You're sure you're okay?"

"I am. Come inside. My students had their parents send me a care package."

"Is that what smells good?"

She nodded. "Can you grab the bags? My head feels like it's going to explode when I bend over."

"Yeah, of course." But instead of turning away he took a step toward her and placed his hand on her cheek. "How are you feeling?" he asked her, studying her face closely. Part of her wanted to close her eyes and savor the feeling of his touch on her skin, but a bigger part of her wanted to remove his hand from her face and push her body closer to his.

But she did neither. She just looked into his concerned dark eyes. "I'm feeling better." She was, really. Better now than she had been feeling all day. There was something about Asa… She couldn't put her finger on it, but there was something about him that made her feel like she was having an out-of-body experience.

"Good. I've been thinking about you all day." His thumb briefly stroked along her cheek, and Hallie swallowed hard as tingles ran down her spine. How could one simple touch be so affecting? "My mother called and asked about you. I promised her I would see how you were." He took a step backward and stripped off his jacket, revealing his powerful arms and chest. As he turned to pick up the bags, she saw how his muscles worked beneath his uniform shirt. She wanted to fan herself. She wasn't used to being around a man with Asa's kind of body. Her ex was much, much different.

"Your mother is very kind to ask about me. I thought you weren't working today." She hadn't meant to say that. But thoughts of him had been on her mind all day, wondering if and when he might show up at her door.

She had told him that she just wanted to be friends but her thoughts about him today hadn't been exactly friendly.

"I got asked to switch shifts." He unloaded the bag on the counter. There was fried chicken, beef patties, a rice dish, and some homemade macaroni-and-cheese among the staples that the parents included. "I now see why you were crying. This food looks amazing."

"Stay with me and have some." She paused. Asa might have kissed her last night, but that didn't mean he didn't have plans with someone else tonight. He was a beautiful man. She would be surprised if he didn't have some woman waiting in the wings. "That is, if you want to, or don't have any other plans."

"I don't." He looked through her cabinets, pulling out plates and glasses. "If you think you're getting rid of me after I smelled this food, you're crazy."

A little bit of pleasure flowed through her. "How was work today? Did you run into any other slip-and-fall victims?"

He grinned. "One this week is enough." He piled the plates high with food and motioned for her to go sit on her couch. "Go sit, I'll bring your food over."

"I can carry a plate." She reached to take one from him.

He gave her a look and shook his head once firmly. "Go sit. I'll bring it over. But tell me what you want to drink first."

"I've got cranberry juice in there. I wish I could offer you something fancier."

He gave her a small smile. "I don't need anything fancy. I'll be there soon."

A few minutes later he had brought their food over and sat next to her on her love seat, his body completely pressed against hers. Suddenly she felt shy. Like she was in high school again, sitting next to the most handsome boy in school. "Were you popular in high school?" she asked as she took her first bite of the rice and pigeon peas.

"Yes. Why do you ask?"

"You just seem like you were. I wasn't. I always had my nose in a book."

"I played football. In my hometown, being on the varsity football team was a very big deal."

"My town was so small we didn't even have a football team. Did you love the game or did you do it just because you knew it would get you girls?"

"A little of both," he admitted with a smile. "I didn't love it as much as my best friend, Marcus. Or at least I thought he loved it. I was sure he was going to go pro but he turned down a few full football scholarships."

"College is so expensive. What made him do that?"

"I'm still not sure. I thought he was crazy. It had something to do with my sister's best friend. They had been secretly in love all through school and broke up right before we graduated."

"So he gave up his scholarship because of that?"

Asa nodded. "He had put the game before her. I guess he was trying to prove something. He worked in public relations in DC until he gave all that up to become a teacher."

"Did they get back together then?"

"Yes, but last year. They met again at my sister's wedding in Costa Rica. They're expecting their first baby."

"Do you see him a lot?" she asked, knowing she was full of questions.

"He lives in New York now, but I don't get to see him as much as I should. He's got a wife and a baby on the way. His life is a lot different than it used to be. We used to catch a plane to Vegas on a whim. Now when I see him, he's planning out how they are going to do their nursery."

"It must be tough, having your friendship change like that." Hallie could identify. Her best friend had had a baby a few months ago, a baby Hallie had never met, but even before that she had been seeing less and less of her friend. Marriage and family often did that.

"It's the way things are supposed to be, though. I would be a selfish bastard if I blamed him for not hanging out with me as much. He's happier now than I have ever seen him. Plus, I love his wife. We grew up together. They're like my family."

"It's nice to have friends like that," she said softly, missing home tremendously then.

"It is." He picked up his glass and took a long drink before he smiled at it.

"Why are you smiling?"

"I was just thinking. Cranberry juice reminds me of Christmas."

"Really? Why? I would think Thanksgiving. Ugh. I was just reminded that I didn't get to have any cranberry sauce this year. Plopping that stuff out of that can is my favorite thing about the holiday."

"My mother hates the stuff from the can and refuses to serve it, but I love it. But cranberries remind me of Christmas because my mother used to make us string them for garland every year."

"That seems like a lot of work," she said, but she could tell by his smile that it was a good memory.

"It was, and my sister and I hated it. But looking back, it was fun. My mother used to go crazy when we were kids. My father would take us to cut down a huge tree every year and my mother would pull out the old ornaments that she got from her grandmother and each one of them had to be placed just right. And in the front, under the star were the ornaments that my sister and I made in first grade. They didn't go with the antique stuff, but they got a place of honor every year."

"That's very sweet. Does she still do that?"

"No." He shook his head and an almost sad expression crossed his face. "She hasn't put up a tree in years. Our house used to be decked out in lights, but after my sister and I graduated from college she stopped doing all of that. It was too much work."

"That doesn't mean you can't do it again. I'm sure your mother would like it if you wanted to do it again."

"She told me they've put the house up for sale and that they are moving to Florida. That's why she stopped by yesterday, to tell me she's retiring. There won't be any more snowy Christmases at that house."

"But what about this Christmas?"

"We're going to my sister's place."

Hallie put her plate down on the table and wrapped her arms around his middle, feeling the need to comfort him. "Your childhood home is something you feel should always be there, isn't it?"

"I didn't realize I'd missed all those little traditions until I knew they weren't going to happen anymore."

"You can make your own traditions, you know. You'll get married and have kids and you'll do things for them like your parents did for you."

"You're right." He draped his arm around her and rested his lips on her forehead. She closed her eyes, liking the closeness, the intimacy she had with him. She had never had this with Brent. They'd never just sat like this, their skin touching, their arms wrapped around each other, each lost in their own thoughts.

The only time Brent touched her was when he wanted to take her to bed. She barely knew Asa and yet was sitting this close to him on the couch. She felt closer to him than the man she had been planning to spend the rest of her life with. And then it dawned on her what she was doing.

She sat up quickly, retrieving her plate so that her hands would be full and not reach for him.

She barely knew him.

They were just supposed to be friends.

She wasn't supposed to feel this kind of pull toward him.

Chapter 5

Asa knocked on Hallie's door two mornings later. She opened it almost immediately and smiled when she saw that it was him. She looked better than he had seen her look all week. The pain and exhaustion that had come over her the last few times he had seen her seemed to have disappeared.

"Hi. I wasn't expecting to see you this morning. I'm just heading out. I have an appointment with my doctor so he can clear me to go back to work next week."

"I know. That's why I'm here." He looked down at her feet to see that she was wearing pink ballet flats. Better than the high-heeled boots she had worn the day she slipped and fell but nowhere near the right footwear for this very cold season. "I need to tell you something important. Can I come in for a moment?"

"Yeah." She looked unsure, but she stepped aside. "What's up?"

"I couldn't in good conscience let you out of the building without wearing the right stuff." He pulled a pair of black fur-lined boots. "Look at the rubber soles on these."

"Oh, Asa." She moaned as she took them from him.

The sound caught him off guard and his groin grew tight. It had been hard for him to be with her the other day and not touch her. He had spent nearly four hours with her that night. They had eaten dinner together and talked about their friends and their college days. They had even watched a Claymation Christmas special that was on. It wasn't a date, but if it had been it would have easily been one of the best he had ever been on. It was nice to come home after a long day of work and have somebody there waiting. And when it was time for him to go, he had to stop himself from pulling her soft, curvy body into his and kissing her until she melted. But he knew if he did that it would have been hard to stop at just a kiss. He would have wanted to tumble her onto her bed and peel every inch of clothing off her, just so he could kiss every inch of her lush bare skin.

He pulled himself out of that fantasy, because he could feel himself growing harder as he thought about her. He didn't need to fantasize about her because the look of pure pleasure on her face would be enough to sustain him for years.

"I've never had a pair of snow boots. These are cute, too."

"I got you something else. Hat, scarf, gloves and an official limited edition FDNY fleece hooded jacket." He pulled them all out of the bag. "It's water resistant, too."

"Asa…" She looked up at him, eyes full of something he couldn't name. Gratitude? Appreciation? He didn't know. He just knew he liked looking into her eyes and when he hadn't seen her at all the day before he'd missed those eyes. He found himself just missing her.

It was odd. He had never felt that way about another woman. He wasn't sure what it was about her, what made her different from anyone else.

“I might cry again. This is the nicest thing any man has ever done for me.”

“It can’t be. Your ex must have done nice things for you.”

“He would buy me a lot of jewelry, but I think it was more for him than me. So he could parade me in front of his wealthy friends and show them what he could afford to buy. But this is…thoughtful. Thank you for being so thoughtful.”

He nodded, wanting to kiss her, but holding back. “Put them on. I can’t let you out on the streets of New York City until you do.”

She sat down on her couch and slipped her feet inside of the boots. She moaned again as her feet touched the warm, soft lining. She was a moaner. She moaned when she ate cupcakes. She moaned when she was pleased. She’d moaned when he had kissed her. He was starting to become addicted to that sound.

“My feet will never be cold again in these.”

“How could you live in New York and not have a good pair of boots?”

“I’m from the South. I didn’t think about it. My cousin told me it was eighty degrees there today. When it gets below fifty-five back home we go into a panic.”

“Southerners.” He shook his head.

“I was stupid. I just didn’t think about it. I didn’t have a winter coat. It was the end of June when I moved here and so unbearably hot that I thought it was never going to cool down. In the back of my mind I knew winter would come. I just didn’t think it would be so cold.”

“This is not typical December weather. It’s one of the coldest on record. We’re responding to a lot of exposure calls. Frostbite, hypothermia. One man didn’t…” He stopped himself, not wanting to expose that detail to her.

"Why did you stop?" She looked suspicious. "What were you going to say?"

"Nothing." He took the scarf and wrapped it around her neck. "Just stay warm today."

"I will. Thanks to you." She stood up. "Would you want to come with me today?"

He grinned at her. "Don't trust yourself outside yet?"

"No." She grinned back. "I haven't been outside in a few days and I don't want to hurry back. I could buy you lunch and take you to a movie. Whatever you wanted to do. It will be my small way of thanking you."

"You don't have to thank me. But I will go to the doctor with you. I don't trust you on the ice, either."

It was only a few blocks to her doctor's office and they decided to walk there. Asa sat in the waiting room thinking about what his life would have been like if he had gone through with becoming a doctor. He would have chosen to be a heart surgeon, or maybe work in emergency medicine. He'd never seen himself in an office like this. He had always liked the fast-paced stuff, the life or death of it all. But he could do that as a rescue paramedic without the residency and certifications and fellowships. His friends thought he was crazy for giving up the prestige and the much higher salary, but what most people didn't know was that he didn't have the need for money. Or the prestige.

He had helped invent a special knee brace with one of his friends that became incredibly popular with athletes. He'd played football all through college. He had stayed incredibly active afterward. He knew how athletes' bodies worked. He knew how they hurt and along with his knowledge of human anatomy and the help of a roommate who was a biomedical engineer, he had come up with something good. His design was used by millions of people. He was nowhere as rich as his brother-in-law, but he'd gained a small fortune when they had sold the design and he still received a percentage of the profits every year. He could have lived a flashier lifestyle. But he liked his fairly simple life.

He had made a choice long ago to not let what he could have influence how he lived his life.

Hallie emerged from the back of the office and he stood up to meet her. "What did the doctor say?"

"He's making me take an extra day. I'm still having issues looking at computer screens."

"It makes your head hurt?"

"The words swim all over the screen."

"Were you trying to do work for school?"

She looked guilty. "Just some emails and light lesson planning."

"Hallie..."

"I've been cooped up in my apartment! I was making use of my time."

"The more you stress your eyes and brain, the longer it's going to take for you to recover. I'm going to make sure you don't do any of that stuff today."

"No?"

"No." He took her hand and led her outside. Today he didn't want her thinking about anything but enjoying herself.

"I can't believe it's snowing again," she said as they stepped outside.

"This is the best kind of snow. Big, fat flakes." He held on to her hand as they navigated the snowy streets. Holding hands wasn't something most friends did, and yet his fingers were locked in hers. She knew she should pull away, but she didn't want to because she liked the way his big, warm hand felt in hers, as if they had been holding hands their entire lives. “Look what it does to the trees.”

He pointed to one as they entered Washington Square Park through a wrought iron gate. Hallie had been a major snow hater since it caused her to miss going home for Thanksgiving, but even she had to admit how beautiful the park was as they walked through it. There was glistening snow on the branches and on the ground all around them. The park was empty on this cold weekday morning and it felt as if they had the entire world to themselves.

“Okay. It is kind of nice.”

“You don’t impress easily, do you?”

“I grew up on the beach with gorgeous powdery sand to wiggle between my toes. I didn’t realize how much I would miss that feeling when I moved here. I could always go to the beach after work and dig my feet in the sand. I can’t dig my feet in the snow.”

“You could. They just might fall off later.” He let go of his hand and wrapped his arm around her. “It doesn’t snow all that much here. You should see upstate. I had a buddy who went to school in Buffalo. They had one hundred and ninety-nine inches of snow one season.”

“No.” Hallie shook her head. “I can’t hear that. I don’t even want to imagine that. Those poor people.”

“They’re used to it. And that’s nothing compared to Alta in Utah. They get six hundred inches annually.”

Hallie felt a little queasy. “That’s terrible. People are afraid of serial killers and zombies, but my worst nightmare is being surrounded by snow with no way to get out.”

“The people who go to Alta love it. It’s a ski town. The very wealthy hang out there.”

“How do you know so much about it?”

“I’ve been.”

“How bourgie of you,” she laughed.

"My father was a high-ranking military official. My mother teaches at a prestigious university and I went to the best medical school in the country. We were exposed to a lot of things that a lot of people never have the chance to see."

"Your parents took you skiing there? Forgive me, but your mother doesn't seem the type to be racing down mountains."

"No. She's not." He shook his head with a smile. "I went with a friend's family while on break from medical school. It was an experience."

"Something you want to repeat again?"

"No. Not a ton of diversity there. That's why I love New York City. Every country in the world is represented here. I can walk out of my apartment and hear five different languages before I get to work. I can see old architecture and new culture and I—"

"—can get a burrito with extra sour cream at three thirty in the morning," Hallie added.

He grinned at her. "That's obviously my favorite part. Along with the hot dogs and the cheesecake."

"And the pizza. Don't forget the pizza."

"That goes without saying. I've spent some time in Chicago and that deep dish stuff doesn't deserve to be called pizza. It's a casserole."

"Those might be fighting words in some places."

"Don't tell me you like deep dish more than traditional?"

"Of course not. My father was born and raised in this city. I could never pledge allegiance to another type of pizza."

"Good. It's bad enough you hate the snow. I don't think we could be friends if you didn't like New York pizza."

"You're my only friend here. I'm not sure I could take

you abandoning me," she said, not meaning it the way it sounded. But there was a little extra heaviness in her voice. It appeared whenever she talked about her father.

"You don't mean that. You must have other friends here. What about the people you work with?"

"Oh, they're nice. But most of them are married with children and when the last bell rings they hurry off to be with their loved ones, which they should. I thought my move here would be easier than it has been. My father talked about this place with such great passion. About how exciting it was. I guess I just wanted to feel some of that."

"What does your father say about it?"

"He passed away. Maybe I came here to feel closer to him. He used to live in this neighborhood. Got his start designing here."

"I'm sorry about your father," Asa said softly.

"Oh, don't be. He died very happy, surrounded by everyone he loved, in his favorite place."

"I'm not sorry for him, Hallie. I'm sorry for you because you are the one who is missing out on his love."

She looked up at Asa, her heart beating just a little harder. He always had a knack for saying just the right thing at the right time. "He would hate for me to be sad. He would be happy that I'm not marrying Brent, though. Hated him. I should have known then."

"Father knows best," Asa said. "What did he design?"

"Buildings. Homes, later in his career. He was an architect."

"Your father was Hal Roberts?"

"You know of him?"

"Your father is a legend, Hallie. He designed that children's museum to look like a medieval castle with a moat and a drawbridge. And the seashell house and the building that looked like a basket and the library that looked like a bunch of giant books. It was brilliant. My mother took us to see some of them."

"But those places are all around the world."

"Yeah. My parents didn't believe in waterparks or arcades. If we were going on vacation, we were going to learn something."

"I'm jealous of you, Asa. I never got to see his work."

"He never took you?"

"No. My father was quite a bit older than my mother. People probably thought she was an opportunist or that he was a dirty old man, but they loved each other in a deep, deep way. My father was a kid at heart and my mother is an old soul. They balanced each other out and when my father retired, he never wanted to leave home. My hometown is so peaceful. He was just so incredibly happy living out his days in the home he built."

"That's a very nice thing." He wrapped his arm around her shoulder and dropped a kiss on her forehead as they continued to walk through the park.

She didn't know where they were going. She didn't bother to ask. She was sure she hated New York, and the cold, and the snow. But right then she was feeling very generous to all three, because she couldn't think of anyplace else she'd rather be in that moment, than with this warm man, in this cold weather with their feet crunching in the snow as they walked to an unknown destination.

They were silent for a long while. Not needing to speak. There was no awkwardness. No rush to fill up the space with noise. She thought the beach was the only peaceful place she could be, but maybe there was something real to her father's love about this neighborhood and this park.

"This is what I wanted you to see." They had stopped in front of that famous arch and in the center of it was a beautiful large evergreen decorated in red lights. "Everyone makes such a big deal about the one at Rockefeller Center, but this is my favorite."

She could see why. There was no one else there, just them, with the snow falling around them in one of the most picturesque places in New York. Not everyone got to see this, especially with a man who was as good as the one she was huddled next to.

It had been a very good day, Asa thought as they turned back onto their street. It was after four. The sun was just starting to go down, blanketing the city in an orangey-red sunset. They had spent all day together. The walk in the park, the long lunch in the little hidden café. He took her to a bakery that his friend owned where they got a tray of holiday desserts that they shared. And they talked some more, while she drank a huge mug of hot chocolate. When they walked back to their apartment building he knew he didn't want the day to end yet.

"Let's get a tree," he said to her.

"What?" She looked up at him, her pretty eyes going wide. Her curls sticking out from under her hat. She was so damn cute. He never thought he had had a type before, but Hallie wasn't the type of woman he usually dated; maybe that was why he was finding himself so incredibly attracted to her. Maybe the fact that she was different was the reason he never wanted his time with her to come to an end.

"There's a lot around the corner. We should get a Christmas tree."

"Right now?" She blinked at him.

"Yeah, right now."

"I don't have any space to put a tree. I can barely fit myself in my apartment."

"We'll put it in my place."

"We don't have any ornaments."

"We'll get some."

"And a tree stand?"

"I'm sure we can buy one of those, too." He took her hand and squeezed it. "Let's get a tree."

"Okay." She smiled at him.

Luckily, the guy at the lot sold stands and there was a little dollar store that sold cheap plastic ornaments. Hallie made Asa wait outside of the corner market with the tree while she ran inside.

"What did you get?" he asked her when she came out.

"Cranberries and eggnog of course. If we're going to do this, we're going to do this right. My father used to make us warm chocolate eggnog with a healthy shot of liquor. We don't have any rum, but it will still be good."

"Baby, we are in luck, because I have a full bar in my place. I've even got whipped cream for the chocolate eggnog."

"I don't want to know why a single, good-looking man has whipped cream in his refrigerator." She gave him a sexy grin. "Maybe I do."

"You'll find out later. Come on. Let's go home."

It was after 9:00 p.m. and they only had half the tree decorated. Hallie was lying on the floor beneath it. She was smiling. Just smiling for no particular reason at all, but Asa was pretty sure it had something to do with the rum they had in their chocolate eggnogs. She'd only had a mug and a half in the few hours they'd been back. But it was enough to make her go all liquidy and giggly.

It made him want to get closer to her. He got on the floor next to her and she reached for his hand, linking her fingers with his. He probably hadn't just held hands with a girl since middle school, but today he found himself reaching for hers a lot.

"What are you doing, Hallie?"

"Just looking up. We've got to get presents to put under this tree, you know. What good is a tree without presents?"

"Did you have lots of presents as a kid?"

"My father used to make me things. Beautiful handmade dollhouses with all the furniture. My favorite was the old Victorian mansion he built for me. It had a little white door and cute little flower boxes in all the windows. They were too nice to play with. He always wanted me to play with them. He told me he would make me as many as I wanted. He said toys were meant to be played with. But they weren't just toys to me, they were works of art. I always knew he was special. He never acted like he was, but I had grown up knowing that my father was one of the most extraordinary people God had ever given to the earth."

Asa rolled on to his side and wrapped his arm around her, bringing them closer. "I hope my kids love me at least a quarter as much as you love your father."

"They will." She sat her hand on his cheek. "Especially if you love their mother."

"I wouldn't make a baby with anyone I didn't love." He slid his hand up her shirt, resting his hand on her side, just so he could feel her skin.

"Easier said than done."

It was true. He had a friend who had gotten a woman that he barely knew pregnant. They weren't compatible. Raising a child with a near stranger was hard for him. So Asa, probably unconsciously, had decided that he was no longer going to sleep with women just to satisfy his need. He was only going to make that step with someone whom he could see raising his children with, that he could see being linked to for the rest of his life.

And yet there was this beautiful woman in his arms, a woman he barely knew and he knew with every fiber in his being that if she wanted to go to bed with him, he would take her and make love to her all night and not think about anything else but making her feel good. "Tell me more about your family."

"It's just my mother's side left, which is big enough. My cousin is my best friend. He's the mayor of our town."

"The mayor?"

"Youngest one we've ever had. He's a do-gooder, too. Donates his salary back to the town. Volunteers at the community center, and when there's a storm he personally goes around town boarding people's windows up. He makes me sick."

Asa laughed and rubbed his nose against her cheek. There was a faint smell of something sweet that he couldn't name, but he found it slightly addictive and buried his nose in the seam of her neck to inhale more of her scent. "I thought he was your best friend."

"He is. But one finds oneself lacking when comparing oneself to such goodness."

"You're being dramatic."

"A little. He's not preachy or sanctimonious about how good he is, either, which makes him even more annoying. He doesn't guilt anyone else. He doesn't ask anyone else to do anything. He just does."

"I think I would like him."

"You would. You're similar men. But Derek has flaws. He's so into giving to everyone else he can't give enough to a woman. Every single woman on the island has thrown herself at him, but he barely seems to notice. He likes divorcées who don't want any commitment from him."

"Why is that a bad thing?"

"Because he deserves someone to love him. I want that for him."

"Maybe he just hasn't found the right woman yet." He

lifted his head to look down at her. "Give him time." He rubbed one of her curls between his fingers. "These things kind of sneak up on a man."

"I like the tree," she said, looking up at it. "I know it's not done but it looks pretty with white lights. Am I talking too much? I think it might be the chocolate eggnog."

"No, it would be the rum in the chocolate eggnog."

She grinned up at him. "You might be right about that. Did you like it?"

"It was good."

"We ate so much today, but I don't care. There's nothing better than being warm, happy and full."

"Are you happy? I was beginning to think you hated being here in New York."

"Spending the day with you made it more tolerable."

"I think that might have been a compliment."

"It was. I can't remember the last time I had a day this good. Thank you for spending it with me."

"Don't thank me." He lowered his mouth to her lips and just rubbed his across her soft, full ones. Her eyes drifted closed. Her body went slack beneath him and he knew there was no stopping what he was going to do next. He kissed her. Beneath the Christmas tree. She tasted like chocolate and spiced rum. That combined with the flavor of her lips made her delicious. It made him greedy and he couldn't stop himself from going back for more and deepening the kiss. She responded by opening her mouth beneath his and welcoming in his tongue.

He didn't need alcohol tonight. He could happily get drunk off her.

She broke the kiss and set her lips on his jawline, sliding them across it and leaving behind little sweet kisses.

He didn't ever think he had been kissed so sweetly in

his life. He didn't ever think he had been this turned on, especially by a woman who was wearing so many clothes.

"You're not supposed to be kissing me, Asa Andersen." Her voice was breathy. Sexy. She had no idea how crazy she was driving him. The sweet little schoolteacher made him want to burst out of his skin.

"You're not supposed to be kissing me back."

"I know. I think you make my brain go to mush when you kiss me and I forget who and where I am."

"You think?"

She grabbed his shirt and pulled him closer to her. "You should kiss me again so I can make sure."

He couldn't describe what he felt when his lips touched hers for the second time that night. A shift? His world being rocked? It was something big, though. Big and exciting. He had jumped out of planes and helped rescue people from collapsed buildings but there was no rush as big as kissing an English teacher underneath a Christmas tree.

She pushed him away. "Yeah." Her eyes were still closed, her lips plump and kiss-swollen. "Mushy brain." She stood up. "We need to finish decorating this tree. It's getting late."

Asa didn't follow. He just continued to lie on the floor, willing his arousal to die down, but he knew it would be a losing battle, because as long as he was anywhere near her it would want her.

And he had a feeling that she was the one woman he would always want.

Chapter 6

The next morning a little after nine, Hallie's cell phone rang. She didn't look at the caller ID, figuring it was her cousin, Derek, calling her as he drove into work for the once-a-week office hours he kept as mayor.

"Hello, cousin."

"It's not your cousin. It's your mother and I'm guessing that the fact that you answered your phone when I know you should be in third period now means you actually are hurt. I'm coming up there! And we're packing your things and you're coming home."

"Mom, no! I'm fine. Don't come up here, and how did you find out I got hurt?"

"Derek let it slip when he was at the house booking your flight home for Christmas."

"He had to book it at your house? What a dummy!"

"He had an alert set up to notify him of a better deal and his phone kept making a god-awful racket. He told me he was looking for flights for you and when I asked him why you weren't looking for your own flight he told me that you were in too much pain to look at a computer screen. And then he clamped his mouth shut, trying to play it off like you just had a headache, but I knew. A mother always knows. I have been feeling off this whole week—I should have figured out sooner that my baby was in trouble."

"I'm not in trouble, Mommy. I promise!" There was a knock on her door and she got up to answer it. "I'll be home soon. You don't have to come here."

It was Asa at the door, looking delicious in a beige cable-knit sweater, jeans and boots. She was dressed in leggings and a cranberry-colored tunic sweater, but she felt grubby next to him. He always looked so handsome. It didn't matter if he had just come home after a twelve-hour shift or was freshly showered and shaved—he was simply gorgeous all the time. He made her feel like a bushel of butterflies was let loose in her stomach. She kept thinking about their kiss beneath the Christmas tree last night. She didn't know if it was the twinkling lights, or the smell of the tree combined with the warm, fuzzy feeling the eggnog had given her, but when Asa settled his hard body on hers, she couldn't help but think that it was all kinds of magical.

It could have been the head trauma talking, but still it was one of those memories she would keep and bring out whenever she was sad or cold or lonely.

"Hallie! Mina, what's the number for 911 in Manhattan?" Her mother, Clara, called to one of her aunts. "Hallie's gone nonresponsive."

"Mom, I'm here. There was a knock at my door."

"Is it a burglar? Do you have your baseball bat?"

"Do you want me to come back later?" Asa asked her.

She shook her head and grabbed Asa's hand, pulling him inside. "Yes, Mom. The bat never leaves my side." She covered the receiver and looked up at him. "You might want to make yourself comfortable. It's going to be a little while."

"Did you get the pepper spray I sent you?"

"I did, and that wasn't pepper spray, that was bear spray." Hallie flopped down on her bed.

"I know. But they told me I couldn't mail you pepper spray and I know you wouldn't go out and buy it yourself. You know I worry about you all alone in that big city and I want you to be as protected as possible."

"I know, Mom. But it comes in a huge canister and is meant to deter an aggressive bear. I'm pretty sure you're not supposed to use it on humans."

"If you had had the bear spray two months ago, you wouldn't have been mugged."

"You were mugged?" Asa came over to the bed and placed half his body on top of hers. There was anger in his face and she found it very sexy. Or it could be the fact that his lower body was pressed between her legs. She had to stop herself from wrapping her thighs around him. She couldn't be thinking these thoughts when her mother was on the phone.

"Who was that?" her mother nearly shouted. "Is there a man in your apartment?"

"No." She put her hand over Asa's mouth. "Must be the TV. I'm watching some cop show. But even if there was a man in my apartment, would you care?"

"Of course I would. It's early in the day, which means he wouldn't have left last night and in that case I would say tell me more. You've been broken up with Brent for a long time."

"Let's not talk about him." She looked up at Asa, who had removed her hand from his mouth and was now lying at her side with one arm draped over her. She had realized why things felt so different with him and it wasn't because he and Brent were such vastly different men. Asa liked to touch her, sit next to her with their skin touching, get closer to her so that their bodies pressed together. He touched her face and locked his fingers with hers and slid his hand up her shirt, not in a sexual way, but just to stroke her skin. She liked that. She could never go back to being with a man who didn't take the opportunity to touch her.

"He's been kind of pathetic, Hallie. I didn't want to tell you before, because he should be mourning the loss of the best thing that had ever happened to him, but he just looks like a lost puppy without you. Moping around downtown. His eyes dull. I feel for him."

"Are you sure he's not just sick?"

"He's sick in love. I think he finally realizes that you were the best part of him. He can't keep his life together without you."

Hallie was getting a little annoyed with this topic. Brent had broken her heart. She didn't care how he was doing, but her mother always made it a point to tell her. "He should hire a personal assistant. I gave up finishing my doctorate for him. I don't care if he's sad, Mom. Please don't tell me anymore."

"He's been asking about you. He called the other day to see if you were coming home for Christmas. He was disappointed not seeing you for Thanksgiving. He said he wants to clear the air with you."

"And I want back the last five years of my life, but that ain't happening anytime soon." Her mother had loved Brent. Hallie had been with him for so long he had become part of her family and she his. Her mother was probably feeling like she had lost a son. But things were really over. There was no going back for them.

"I don't tell you this because I want you to speak to him. I'm just telling you this because it means he really does love you. He was talking out of his behind when he said those things to you. He probably just had cold feet."

"It sounds like you want me to forget everything that happened and get back together with him."

"I think he might have changed. He wants to settle down here and make a life with you. And I want you to come home and never leave me again."

"Mom...."

"I only have you, Hallie. You're my baby. The only piece of your father that I have left, and I would die if anything happened to you. Keel over and die. Drop dead on the spot with grief."

"Mom, please stop being so morbidly dramatic."

"I'm not. Hallie, I know you need to do this for yourself and I want desperately for you to be happy, but I just miss you. You're not just my kid, you're my best friend."

Hallie felt her heart squeeze painfully then. "I love you, too, Mom. Can we talk about this more when I come home for Christmas?"

"Yes, of course. Are you sure you are feeling okay?"

"I slipped on ice on my way to work Monday and hit my head. I have a little bit of a concussion, but I'm feeling fine for the most part. A really beautiful paramedic came to my rescue. And my neighbor looks in on me. You don't need to worry."

"You do realize that it's never going to stop, right?"

"I do. I'll speak to you later, Mom."

"Okay, baby. Goodbye."

Hallie dropped her phone and inched closer to Asa, glad he was there to lean against. "My mother is the queen of guilt. If there were gold medals given out for the sport she would hands down win."

"I heard." He kissed her temple. "It's good to have someone love you that much."

"I'm going to have to give her grandchildren fairly soon."

"Oh, about four or five to start."

Hallie laughed, but she knew that she didn't see herself spending the rest of her life here. She didn't see herself raising her children far away from their grandmother, or the place where she felt most connected to the grandfather that they would never meet.

"Would you come with me today?" Asa asked. He sounded a little subdued. She felt there was a slight shift in his mood.

"Yes," she answered without hesitation. "You're not working today?"

"No. I have the next two days off. I've been working a lot of overtime. You didn't ask me where I wanted you to go."

"I trust you."

"Maybe you shouldn't. We won't get back till late tonight and this trip might require you to bring extra clothes."

"Are we going on some kind of heist?" She rubbed his arm. "I don't think I'm limber enough to avoid those laser motion detectors."

"No? I would like to see you wiggle around in a black cat suit, though."

"What's the matter, Asa?"

"You were mugged?"

"It wasn't like I was held up at gunpoint. This skinny hipster guy came up to me and asked me if I had the newest iPhone. I told him I did and he took it out of my hand and ran off."

"I fully endorse your mother giving you bear spray."

"Of course you do."

"You want to go out for breakfast first? I know a place near the lot where I keep my car."

"We're going someplace we need to drive?"

"Yes." He kissed the side of her neck. "Unless you want to stay here. I'm comfortable where I am."

It would be easy to stay in bed with him all day. In fact it was something she could see herself doing. She really liked Asa. She was more attracted to him than she had been to anyone else, but she was still hurting about Brent. Not because she missed him, not because there was still love there, but because she had planned so much of her life around him. And he'd hurt her, more than she thought it was possible. She could fall in love with Asa. It would be too easy to. But she couldn't take another heartbreak.

If the breakup with Brent threw her for a loop when she knew it was ultimately for the best, she wouldn't be able to survive another loss. But that didn't mean she could pull herself away from Asa. It didn't mean she wasn't going to spend time with him every chance she got.

"We're going out today. I could use some pancakes." She rolled away from him. "Do you think they'll make reindeer ones for me?"

"You ate so healthy at breakfast," Hallie said to him as they walked to where he kept his car. "I'm a little disappointed. I thought you would eat some kind of lumberjack or hungry-man thing. But you had egg whites and spinach and turkey sausage."

"I'm a rescue paramedic, which means I train with the fire department and perform high-stakes rescues. I have to stay in shape for it. And after yesterday, I needed something green to balance out all the cake and chocolate and beef I had."

"You make me feel guilty for ordering extra bacon."

He grabbed her hand and pulled her into a hug. "Eat bacon. Eat pancakes. Eat whatever you want as long as you feel this good against me. I find you incredibly sexy. Did you know that?"

She tilted her head and looked up at him like she wasn't sure whether to believe him or not. "No one has ever called me sexy before."

"The man who failed to tell you that you were sexy is a complete and total jackass." That was the man who was still apparently in love with her, who was still moping around town like a lost dog.

He had listened to every word of the conversation she'd had with her mother and he hated it. He hated that someone had broken her heart so badly that she had to move hundreds of miles away from her family. He hated that she felt unlovable.

She reached up to kiss him, surprising him when she looped her arms around his neck and rubbed her chest against his. She was lucky that they were in a garage and far away from a bed because he was finding it harder and harder to resist her. "Asa, stop kissing me!"

"I didn't—"

She pressed her lips to his again. "Let me pretend and blame you for this," she spoke without removing her mouth from his. "I can tell myself later that you kept kissing me and I couldn't help but kiss you back."

"Why do you have to tell yourself that?" he asked as she continued to kiss him. Small full-lipped pecks that made it hard for him to concentrate. "You should kiss me if you want to kiss me."

"I could fall in love with you and I don't want to."

They both froze and he pulled away from her slightly to look her in the eye. He was surprised to hear those words. Maybe a little jolted by them, because he could see himself falling in love with her, too.

He had experienced a lot in his life but he had never been in love before.

"I shouldn't have told you that, but I did and it's the truth."

It was too soon, but he was glad that she had told him. There was no pretense, no games with them, and as much as he wanted to give in to whatever this was he knew that half of her heart was still in her hometown. She wanted to go back. There was no use falling for a woman who wasn't going to stay.

"Did I freak you out by saying that?"

"No." He shook his head and then stepped forward, took hold of her face and kissed her deeply. She moaned.

She broke the kiss and rested her head on his shoulder. "Asa, maybe it's not a good thing for us to spend the day together."

"Get in the car." He wasn't going to make things easier for her. It might be too much for them. It might be crazy, but it was worth it to try. He would never forgive himself if he didn't see where this went.

He slipped the key fob out of his pocket and hit the unlock button. His headlights flashed and Hallie stepped away from him. "This is your car?"

"Yes."

"This is a BMW SUV."

"Yes."

"Are you embezzling from the city? Are you taking kickbacks? Or maybe you're some kind of drug lord..."

"Because paramedics don't make enough money to buy BMWs?"

"Yes."

"Would you believe me if I told you my father got me a deal on this car?"

"Yes, but I think there is more to the story."

"When I was in medical school I lived with a biomedical engineer who was going for his master's, and for his final school project we collaborated on a functional knee brace that a lot of athletes use. We sold the design and I get royalties from it."

She stepped forward and set a light kiss on his lips. "Goody Two-shoes." She sighed. "Let's get this day over with."

"You sound like this is going to be a chore."

"No." She said as she opened the door. "I know it's going to be the opposite of that."

Asa had taken her out of the city, which surprised her. She wasn't sure where they were going and she still hadn't asked, but she was enjoying the ride. Just like she was going to enjoy her time with Asa. They hadn't talked for a while, Hallie content to listen to the Christmas songs on the radio as she watched the scenery change. There were no mountains in Florida, just flat land, and there certainly wasn't snow. Hallie had thought Hideaway Island was the most beautiful place in the world and in a way, it was, but her eyes nearly hurt now from all the beauty around her. Huge mountains with snowy peaks and hundreds and hundreds of evergreen trees. There was so much space all around them and it seemed to go on and on like this part of the world was never-ending. As Asa turned off the highway and through the town to get to their destination, Hallie saw large rustic-looking homes that were all decorated for the season. Red bows and Santa Clauses. Fully attired snowmen in the yard. It wasn't dark yet so she couldn't see the lights but she could just imagine how these houses looked when illuminated.

If this wasn't enough to put one in the Christmas spirit nothing could.

Asa pulled to a stop in the parking lot of a train station. "I'm pretty sure we could have caught a train out of Grand Central."

"Not this one." He smiled.

Before them was an old-fashioned diesel locomotive with wreaths hanging in the windows.

"I've never been on a train before." She shook her head, feeling a little choked. "I've been on the subway before, but then I spend most of the time trying to make sure no one is groping me. This is a real train, though." She looked back to him. "This is beautiful."

"I only take the prettiest women with concussions on train rides."

She smiled at him. "And to think if I had worn the right footwear, we wouldn't be here now."

They got out of the car and walked up to the train where a conductor in an old-fashioned uniform greeted them with a warm smile. "Welcome aboard the Christmas Express! Can I see your tickets?" Asa slipped a piece of paper out of his pocket and handed it to him. "Oh, Diamond Class." The conductor looked at Hallie and gave her a playful wink. "Your gentleman must be very fond of you."

Hallie glanced back at Asa who was looking at her as if he was trying to gauge her reaction to all of this. She couldn't help but smile again. She had been doing that a lot lately. She had told him earlier that she didn't want to fall in love with him. It was going to be damn hard not to. She was already as fond of him as one person could get.

Once they were on the train they were shown to their seats in the front. Hallie thought there might be a lot of children on a train ride like this, but as they headed to their seats, she saw that there were families with bouncing children and squirmy toddlers, groups of teenagers, and young couples as well as elderly ones on dates. They all seemed to be buzzing with electricity.

It must have been the ambience. The train's walls were covered in rich wood with brass trim detailing. There were huge picture windows and plush-looking red leather seats that looked comfortable enough to curl up and fall asleep in. It was almost as if they'd been transported back in time. They stopped at the very front of the train where they were seated across from each other at a small table covered by a red-and-green-checked tablecloth. There was a little partition behind her, closing them off from the people behind them. It was intimate and semi-private. The train hadn't even taken off yet and she knew she was going to enjoy this trip very much.

"When did you do this all, Asa? This couldn't have been a spur-of-the-moment thing."

"Last night after you left. I had been hearing about this for a while from a bunch of people. Even my brother-in-law mentioned taking my sister here. I looked it up and saw that there were tickets left and here we are."

"You asked me this morning. What if I had said no, or told you I was busy?"

"Then I would have found some other woman on the street to take. Or better yet, Ms. Peabody in 4C. She's been giving me the eye lately."

"She's eighty-two!"

"She gets around," he countered and she laughed.

The train started to pull off and they traveled farther into the mountains.

"See how great New York is?" he said to her as they looked out the window. "You get everything in one state. The excitement of the city. The beauty of the mountains. In the summertime I can take you to the beach."

She almost started to say she didn't know if she was going to be here in the summer. She knew once she went home for Christmas it would be much harder to come back here and be virtually alone when her family was all there on Hideaway Island. But she stopped herself, because she couldn't say for sure what she was going to do. "You sound like you work for the tourism board."

"I get twenty percent for every out-of-towner I get to move here." He flashed her a grin before he sobered. "I know how hard it must be for you to be away from your family now. I just want to take your mind off things."

"Thank you. I moved here to take my mind off my past and to reevaluate my future. I don't think I succeeded in doing any of those things."

"You're still in love with your ex?"

Her breath caught when he asked her that. She didn't expect the question to come from him and she was even more surprised with the answer that came out of her. "No." She shook her head. "I'm not in love with him anymore. But sometimes I think I still love him. Or what we used to be."

Hallie thought for a moment that maybe she shouldn't be talking about this with Asa, but he reached across the table and grabbed her hand. "You were together a long time."

"It was good for the first few years. It really was. That's how I convinced myself that I wasn't a complete idiot for devoting so much of my life to him. He was sweet and kind and he really did love me. But his career became so important. Too important. He was closing twenty-million-dollar deals. He would go through dark moods if a buyer backed out, but I dealt with it. I tried to help him in any way that I could but it was never good enough."

"He could have changed."

"Maybe." She shrugged. "But I did, too. I made a promise to myself that I wouldn't go backward. I won't. I put him first for years. It's time to put me first."

"I love it when a woman wants to come first," Asa said with a small grin.

His little dirty joke made her really laugh. She couldn't remember the last time she had done so. Not since she had been in New York. Not in the months before it. She had just been existing, but these past few days she had felt like she was living, experiencing things she had never thought she would.

"You make me happy, Asa." She froze after she said it. She was always saying things to him that she didn't mean to say, but everything she said to him was the truth. She had never been so honest with a man in her life.

And if she were honest with herself, she knew that she wouldn't be able to resist him much longer. She was going to have to make love to him. The potential damage to her heart be damned.

Chapter 7

It was snowing when they got off the train, which looked beautiful when they were enclosed in the warmth of the train and had mugs of gourmet hot chocolate in their hands. But when Asa saw his car covered in about five inches of snow, he wasn't so thrilled. Although Hallie seemed to be fine with it. That surprised him. She had been so anti snow and winter, but now she was walking toward the car with her head thrown back to catch the snowflakes hitting her face.

"I feel like I'm in a snow globe," she said, laughing.

This was no gently falling snow like they had experienced the day in the park. It was small, quickly accumulating flakes that reminded him of other storms he had experienced growing up in New Jersey.

"I checked the forecast this morning," he said more to himself than her. "It wasn't supposed to snow."

"You live in the city, don't you?" A man with his family in tow asked.

"How did you know?"

The man grinned. "We get all the snow up here. It's not supposed to get better until later tonight. There's a little resort about two miles up the road with a nice restaurant. Take your wife there. If you pay for the day pass they'll let you hang out and enjoy the amenities all day."

"Thanks for the suggestion. I think I'll do that." He looked over at Hallie again. The man had mistaken her for his wife. It wasn't the first time that had happened today. He wondered if she'd noticed and if she had, did it bother her?

He'd never corrected the assumption. He liked hearing it, that people looked at them and thought they belonged together, that they had made that ultimate commitment.

She had told him that he made her happy. He wanted to keep making her happy. He wanted to keep her in his life.

He grabbed her hand, finding her fingers warm. "You hungry?"

"I could eat." She squeezed his hand. "Thank you for that, Asa. I didn't know it was something I wanted to do until the moment I saw that train."

She didn't have to thank him. Seeing her smile was enough of a thank-you for him. He took his key fob out of his pocket and hit the button for the automatic starter. "It was my pleasure. Go sit in the car. It should be warm soon. As soon as I get the snow cleared off the car we'll be on our way."

"I'll help you," she said, reaching into his car to pull out a snow brush. "It's something that I will add to my lists of New York firsts."

"What else is on your list?" He pulled out his second brush and worked on his side of the car.

She looked upward as if she was thinking about it. "Um. I want to do all those corny touristy things that most real New Yorkers don't even do, like go to the Empire State Building. And I want to see the ballet. My hometown has a tiny dance studio that performs every year, but I would really like to see the professionals do it just once."

"What else?"

"Eat those hot dogs they sell on the street." She looked embarrassed.

"You've never done that?"

"No. I've been afraid to."

He grinned at her. "You haven't lived until you've had one." He cleaned the snow off the roof of his car while she focused on the windshield and soon they were on their way to the resort.

Asa hadn't known what to expect when he pulled up to the resort, but a castle certainly wasn't it. Or porters and bellhops in full throwback uniforms.

"Are you sure we're in the right place, Asa?"

He looked over at Hallie to see her eyes wide with wonder. "I think we are. This is the end of the road."

"I'm dreaming, right? I start off my day on an old train and end up in a castle. I must be dreaming."

"Then I'm dreaming right alongside you."

"You didn't plan this?"

He shook his head. He wished he'd had the foresight, but he would have never taken her here. The train ride was one thing, but taking a woman he had known for just a week away to a resort like this would have been a lot by anyone's standards. But they were here now, seeking shelter from a storm, and it seemed like this was where they were meant to be.

"I was going to take you snow-tubing. That's why I told you to bring a change of clothes, but then I thought that sending a woman recovering from a head injury flying down a slippery hill wasn't the best idea."

She grinned at him. "You really want me to fall in love with snow?"

"No. Just hate it a little less." And he wanted to give her more firsts, be with her when she experienced new things. He kept thinking about how she'd said that she didn't want to fall in love with him. But the potential for it was there and if she could make him feel this good just by liking him, he could only imagine what it would feel like to be loved by Hallie Roberts.

The valet walked up then, breaking him off those thoughts and soon he and Hallie were walking through the lobby of the large historical hotel. He had traveled a lot, but he had never been to a place like this and while he knew he should be taking it all in, he was too busy looking at Hallie. Whose eyes were wide and head was bent back as she took in all the details.

It had been like this while they were on the train. Her eyes had been glued to the scenery as they passed by it, and Asa couldn't take his eyes off her now. He noted every change in her face, every expression of excitement and wonder and happiness. But he had to admit to himself that he would have been as enthralled if they had never left her apartment. He always had a hard time pulling his eyes off her. Surely he must have seen a more beautiful woman, but there had never been another woman he wanted to see as much as the one before him.

She wandered to the stand that displayed the day's activities. "Look, Asa." She took his hand. "It says here that they have an endurance contest for athletes. I'm sure he can show us to a flaming pit of fire that you can jump over or some barbed wire you can crawl through."

"Only if you crawl through the barbed wire with me."

She grinned at him for a moment. "There's also gingerbread house decorating. And a covered ice-skating pavilion. And tea and cookies at four with Christmas carolers. Oh, and they're showing *Die Hard* in their theater."

"*Die Hard*?"

"One of the best Christmas movies ever made. One of the best movies ever made, period."

"You like action movies?"

"I love them, and my mother has a weird thing for Bruce Willis, so I've seen every single one of his movies more than once. Don't ask about who my mother is attracted to. She has very eclectic taste in men."

"I won't, but it is kind of interesting." He grabbed her by the hips and pulled her into him. "Let's not do the day pass. Let's get a room while we're here."

"Okay." She wrapped her arms around him. "You really want to stay for that movie, don't you?"

He chuckled and dropped a kissed on her forehead. "No, but the snow doesn't seem like it's stopping anytime soon and I don't want to push you too hard. I know you're still healing. You should have a place to rest. Maybe take a nap. We can still go home tonight if the snow slows down."

She pressed her lips to his. "You're thoughtful." She kissed him again. "And kind. I'm not sure I know how to handle it."

"Handle being treated like you're supposed to be treated? Hallie, I'm not doing anything special."

"Yes, you are, Asa. You have to have a major flaw. You should let me know what it is right now and make it easier for me."

He shook his head. He did have flaws, but he wasn't going to make it easier for her. He wasn't going to be satisfied until he had all of her and that meant her heart, too. "Come on, let's see what kind of damage we can do in this hotel."

He was trying to make her fall in love with him. Hallie shook her head, looking at Asa as he lounged on the bed in their suite. He didn't just get a simple room. He'd gotten them a suite overlooking the lake with an enormous fireplace and a hot tub in the middle of the room. But it wasn't the luxurious or cozy surroundings that would make her fall. It was just him. Being with him was easy. He made a gingerbread house with her. And genuinely enjoyed himself. There was no begrudging acceptance. No macho pride. He wore a white apron and piped icing on the roof and it was one of the sexiest things she had ever seen. She had never been with a man who was so secure.

Could she even say she was with him? She wasn't. She had to keep reminding herself that she hadn't even known him a week yet. But she had spent nearly every day with him since she had hurt herself. Hours and hours of time. She had met his mother. He had seen her at her worst. From the outside, people might see them as strangers, but she felt like she had known him for a lifetime and she still wanted to know more about him.

"You impressed me today with your ice-skating moves," she said to him as he flipped through the hotel's brochure. "You should have stayed out there longer."

"Nobody wants to skate by themselves."

"Me and ice don't get along."

"No, but if you did we wouldn't be here right now."

She walked over and sat at the foot of the bed. "No. Maybe I should send it a thank-you letter."

He gave her a smile that made her heart beat a little faster. The romance of this room wasn't lost on her. There was a fire roaring in the fireplace. A bottle of wine chilling on the nightstand and the huge bed that looked perfect for two people to get to know each other better in. She wanted him. She wanted him so bad she almost ached for him, but she couldn't accuse him of trying to seduce her.

The snow had slowed down enough for them to drive

home, but she was the one who suggested they stay. He hadn't tried anything besides his normal touches, a simple caress of her arm, his hand on the small of her back, his fingers locked with hers. He was a perfect gentleman and she knew if she told him that she didn't want to do anything but sleep in this big bed that he would be okay with it.

But she wasn't going to tell him that tonight.

"Do you want to head down for dinner? Or are you still full from all that candy you put in your mouth instead of on your gingerbread house."

"They had gummy bears. Pineapple ones, too. Those are my favorite. I wish they just sold them separately so I wouldn't be forced to eat those inferior flavors, too."

"Inferior? You're being a bit harsh, don't you think?"

"Maybe." She grinned at him. "Maybe we should just order something to be sent to the room. I'm not sure if I have enough energy to go back downstairs."

Asa sat up, the concern in his eyes back. "I knew we shouldn't have crammed so much stuff in today. You're still not fully recovered."

"I'm fine. I'm appropriately tired after a good day. We played with candy and walked around the barn museum. It's not like I plowed a field or anything."

"No, but I watched you beat that old man at chess. You were pretty ruthless."

"That old man was a physics professor. I was raised by an old man and they are tricky. Don't let that tweed jacket fool you. That man was out for blood."

"I like that you're competitive. Maybe I can convince you to do a mud run with me in the summer."

"Ha! I don't think so. Unless you're going to challenge me to competitive s'mores making or extreme sleeping, which I will gladly participate in."

"What do you want for dinner?" He picked up the phone on the nightstand.

"Surprise me." She stood up. "I'm going to the bathroom."

She left him alone. It wasn't lost on her that neither one of them had anything to sleep in. She had a change of clothes in her bag for the morning, but tonight she was going to go to sleep in that bed next to him and the thought of her skin touching his was enough to send a rush of tingles throughout her body.

She took off her socks, leggings and bra, emerging from the bathroom in her long sweater. Asa's eyes snapped to her. She had felt his eyes on her a lot today, but the way he was looking at her now was different. He looked at her legs. She wouldn't say they were her best feature. They weren't long and slender by any stretch of the imagination, but the way Asa was looking at them, she felt as sexy as a showgirl.

She climbed back on, taking her spot again at the foot of the bed. "What did you order?"

"A bunch of stuff. A club sandwich, a burger, quesadillas, chocolate lava cake. It should be here soon."

She crawled closer to him and took his hand, stroking his large warm palm. "That sounds perfect."

"What are you doing,?"

"Getting closer to you. I had to sit across from you on the train, and at lunch. There were people around us all day and the only thing I really wanted was to feel your warm, heavy body close to mine like it was this morning before we left."

"Like this?" He had her on her back, his large body on top of hers. His hand cupping the back of her thigh. He squeezed it and her nipples tightened.

"You smell good." She buried her nose in his throat and

then kissed him, pressing her lips to his Adam's apple. "Clean."

It was intoxicating. His scent was arousing and calming at the same time and she was pretty sure she was becoming addicted to him.

"Clean? My mother will be glad to hear that I'm still bathing regularly."

"No expensive, overwhelming cologne. Just clean, warm man. They should bottle this scent."

"I don't know what's going on between us," he said just before he kissed her. She shut her eyes and sunk into the bed as he gently explored her mouth. It was like her body was sighing, like it had been waiting all day for his lips to touch hers. It was just lips at first, but his tongue swept in, just when she needed it to, and he deepened the kiss. This was usually the place where she stopped him, when her core went all liquidy and it felt a little too good. But she wasn't pushing him away this time. She wanted more of this, more of him.

She pulled up his sweater. He had a T-shirt tucked into his pants but she pulled it out, needing to run her hands over his hard back.

"I thought you just wanted to be friends."

"I do, but I think I need this more."

He looked at her for a moment. His eyes searching her face. "I don't want to be your rebound guy."

She just shook her head. This wasn't a rebound. At least, it didn't feel like one to her. She didn't want to sleep with Asa to get over Brent. She had changed jobs. She had moved states away. Her life was different. She was different and she wasn't hung up on her ex. She was just afraid of things not working out with Asa. The last thing she wanted or needed was another heartbreak. Her head was telling her to be careful, but her body, her heart was telling her to give her all to him. "Don't stop now, Asa."

"Once I start I won't be able to stop."

He was looking at her so intensely that her breath caught.

"I want you to be sure about this. No regrets."

She took his face in her hands and pulled him into a kiss. She wouldn't have any regrets, but she would be lying if she said there wasn't a little fear there. She could already feel herself falling for him and she wasn't the type of woman who could separate love and sex. She didn't do casual relationships, and she wasn't sure she wanted to be involved in another serious one so soon. She missed Hideaway Island. She missed her family and when things ended with Brent she promised herself she would finish her doctorate and get the job she had always wanted and do all the things she wasn't able to do while she was being a superambitious man's partner.

And then there was Asa. What did he want from this? Maybe she was overthinking it, but she was wondering if she should ask him. What did he want to happen after tonight? It had to be more. He couldn't have gone through all the trouble he went through just to sleep with her. He was a beautiful man. He could have whatever woman he wanted.

But then his hand slid up her thigh and came to rest on her behind and she stopped thinking. She wrapped her legs around him and gave in to the sensation of being kissed.

She was just about to pull off his sweater when he broke the kiss and left her completely alone on the bed. "We have to stop now."

"Why? What happened?" She sat up feeling bewildered.

"Nothing. The food is here."

"Oh." She collapsed backward on the bed. She was hungry, all right, but this time it wasn't for food.

Chapter 8

Hallie Roberts knew how to drive a man crazy, Asa thought for the twentieth time that night. She kept touching him, and if there was any space between them she inched closer till their bodies were touching. And he loved every second of it. She was seductive without trying to be. Everything she did turned him on, the way she ate and laughed and walked around the room in just a sweater. He wanted to groan.

But it was the way she kissed him that had him nearly shaking with need for her. She didn't hold back. She had wrapped her legs around him and moved against him and he had been so aroused he wasn't sure he was going last longer than two seconds with her. He was glad the food came when it did. It gave him a chance to think, to breathe. It couldn't just be one night with them. That was why he was asking her if she was sure; that was why he wanted her to go into this with open eyes. No other woman made him feel anything near what she made him feel and he wasn't going to give her up soon.

He understood why her ex was pining for her after eight months. The man was stupid to mistreat her, and Asa knew he wasn't going to make the same mistake. He just had to keep his thoughts clear. He didn't want things to get too hot too fast and then just burn out.

He wanted to take his time with her, but it was going to be nearly impossible.

She had left him alone on the bed after barely eating any of the food he had ordered. He wondered for a moment if she was feeling okay but she hadn't acted any differently. Now she was at the hot tub that was perfectly positioned near the fireplace. "I've never been in one of these before," she said as she turned on the faucet.

"No?"

"I keep telling you all of the things I've never done before. You must think I've lived a terribly sheltered life."

"I don't. I like seeing the look on your face when you experience something for the first time."

"Is it childlike wonder?" she asked, grinning.

"No. There is nothing childlike about you." He got up and sat in the overstuffed easy chair by the fireplace to be closer to her. She was now lounging on the side of the tub, her fingers in the water. "Why didn't you eat more? I wouldn't have ordered so much."

"It won't go to waste." She stood up and reached beneath her sweater to pull off her underwear. His mouth went dry and his erection returned in full force. "I'm sure we'll be hungry later. I didn't eat much for vanity reasons." She pulled the sweater off over her head to reveal her nude body. "I wanted to look good for you when I did this."

"Do you think eating a few more French fries would have changed how attracted I am to you? I wanted you when you were dazed from knocking your head. I wanted you when you were in an old bathrobe and thick socks. I want you when you're fully dressed and in a winter coat.

I want you all the time because you are beautiful and you make me smile and I just like being with you."

He saw emotion fill her eyes but she quickly blinked it away. She turned away from him, giving him a phenomenal view of her behind, and stepped into the hot tub. "Take off your clothes, Asa, and come here."

He shut his eyes briefly and took a deep breath. There was nothing more in the world he wanted to do than go to her. But he gripped the chair and braced himself. "I need to tell you something."

"Well, it can't be that you're a woman because I know for a fact you're not. I've felt just how manly you are before the food came."

"It's not that." He opened his eyes and looked at her.

"You're a virgin." She grinned at him and it made her even sexier. "I can work with that. It will be nice for me to show you something for the first time."

He groaned. "I don't have a condom."

"I don't believe you. You brought me up here. You rented this suite. You have been seducing me all day. All week. You have to have one."

"I didn't plan this. I promise you I didn't."

"Of course not. You really are just that thoughtful without wanting anything in return. And that makes me want you even more. Go get a condom. Go get a box of condoms."

"The gift shop closed at eight. I didn't realize that there wasn't one in my wallet until I went to tip room service."

She let out a slow breath. "Get naked and come here anyway. It will be like high school. I think we can have fun just touching."

He rose slowly from his chair. He wasn't that strong a man. He had a lot of willpower, but not when it came to her. He stripped off his sweater and T-shirt, watching her as she watched him with hungry eyes.

"Dreams do come true," she said.

"Excuse me?" he asked as his hands went to his belt buckle.

"I dreamed about you taking off your clothes in front of me like this. Every night since we've met. You're better than my dreams."

He finished undressing and stepped into the hot, bubbling water. He had been in a lot of hot tubs, especially after his football practices, trying to soothe his aching muscles. It had been so many that they had lost their appeal. There had been nothing sexy about them until right now, and that was because he was going to get to spend time in one with Hallie.

She reached him and wrapped her arms around him, pressing her breasts to his chest. He moaned. It was her soft naked body, the heat or the water, combined with the way her wet skin felt beneath his fingers that made this one of the most erotic moments of his life. He was so hard he couldn't see straight.

His kissed the side of her neck and then her shoulder. "I have wanted to get in the tub with you ever since that day you took a bath at my place."

"I was half hoping you would try to get in the tub with me."

"You were suspicious of me, if I recall correctly. What would you have done if I'd tried to?"

"I don't know. I really wanted to know what you looked like naked. I've never seen so many abs." She ran her hand down his stomach. "I think I would have seen these and forgotten to be cautious."

"Are you telling me that any guy flashes his abs and you're putty in his hands?"

"No. That's the crazy thing. I made Brent wait forever to see me naked, and I do mean forever. We dated in high school and he got nowhere with me. We broke up before we went to college and then got back together when I moved back home, and I made him chase me for months."

"You made him earn your love. Nothing wrong with that."

"He was always so used to getting what he wanted when he wanted it. I wasn't going to be that for him, too."

"I can wait for you," he told her as he ran his hand down her back. "We can take as long as you want."

"I don't want to wait and that's why this scares me. I'm feeling too much, too fast."

She was right. If he stopped to think about it, this was insane. He had known her a week. It felt like a lifetime, but it was less than a week, and he was thinking about the future, about not wanting to let her go. "Let's think about it another way. When you're dating someone new, how often do you see them?"

"About once a week."

"How long do your dates last?"

"A few hours."

"How much do you talk to them during the week?"

"I don't know, maybe once or twice for a few minutes."

"Now think about us. I've seen you almost every day this week. If you just count up yesterday and today we've spent at least twenty-four hours together and at least four hours every other day this week. You've been to my place. You've met my mother. I'd say we're where most people might be three or four months down the line. And if anyone asks you can say we've been neighbors for months."

She gave him a soft smile before she kissed him. It was one of those hot kisses that made him nearly lose control. It made him forget where he was —upstate in a beautifully done hotel suite and in a hot tub with her. Everything else faded away, all thoughts faded away. It was just her mouth on his. Her body pressed against his. He wanted to be inside of her so badly.

Maybe it was meant to be that he didn't have protection. Maybe it was a sign to slow down, to get to know her body, to give her pleasure without needing anything in return.

She made him feel like a teenager, hyper-aroused all the time. But even the sex-crazed sixteen-year-old boy he used to be had never wanted a woman this much.

He broke the kiss and looked at her. She gave him an almost shy smile and it hit him hard in the chest. She didn't hold back. He knew she was going to give him her all.

"Turn around."

She blinked at him, but then did as he asked. Her gorgeous round bottom brushed against his manhood and it jumped. She noticed and rubbed herself against him and he hissed out a breath.

"Behave yourself." His voice came out thick, choked. He was using every ounce of his willpower to control himself.

"I want to make you feel good, Asa."

"Then sit still and let me touch you."

She relaxed into him, her head coming back to rest on his shoulder. The water made her buoyant, her legs floated up, but he kept her body close to his by wrapping his arm around her and running his hand down her side. She was curvy and for days he had longed to run his hand down her waist and stroke the round hips that made her so womanly.

Her eyes drifted shut and she let out a long sigh, encouraging him to continue his exploration of her body. He touched her stomach, loving how her softness contrasted with his hardness. His fingers wandered up her torso, slid in between her breasts and he heard her breath quicken. He paused there, placing his palm flat over her heart.

"Asa…" she moaned.

"What?" He moved his hand down to her breast, cupping it in his hand and squeezing slightly.

"Let me touch you."

"No." He ran his thumb over her nipple, then rolled it between his fingers, tugging on it.

Hallie bit her lip. It aroused him even further, which at this point he thought was impossible.

She turned in his arms before he could stop her and straddled him, taking his member in her hand and stroking it.

"It's not your turn." He stood, causing her to grab on to him, and stepped out of the hot tub. There was a window seat filled with cushions and pillows. He deposited her there. Their bodies were wet, but the room was nice and warm from the roaring fire. He knelt on the seat between her legs, his hands on her shoulders not allowing her to turn the tables. "I'm not done yet."

Her eyes were full of need. He took pleasure in that as he bent his head to kiss her chest. Warm, wet skin. His lips glided over it. He kissed the side curve of her breasts then the undersides of them before he licked across her nipples. She writhed beneath him. Her fingers dug into his arms, but he wouldn't let up. He opened his mouth, taking her entire areola inside. He sucked on her, changing his pressure, taking note of her every breath, moan and reaction. He wanted to make this good. He wanted to make this something she wanted more of.

"Asa…"

He kissed his way down her body, spreading her legs wider as he moved lower. He nipped the inside of her thigh, and then soothed it with a flick of his tongue.

"Stop playing with me," she begged. This time he obeyed. He slid his fingers over her lower lips, finding her wet, ready for him and so he opened her and tasted, taking one long lick.

She cried out, saying some words he didn't understand and he took that as encouragement. He licked deeper, slipping his fingers inside of her. She started to tremble then; the buildup was coming. She wasn't passive. She moved with him. She cried out his name, she gave him as much pleasure as she was getting even though she wasn't touching him at all.

The explosion that came from her was amazing and he couldn't take his eyes away from her face. She was so damn beautiful.

He rested his head on her belly while she recovered. After a while he felt her fingers on his face, stroking his cheek with her thumb. "Asa?"

"Hmm?" He was hard as a rock, but he felt sleepy and satisfied at the same time. It wasn't something he had experienced before.

"You're very good at that."

He kissed her belly. "I aim to please."

"I do, too. Get up. It's my turn now."

Chapter 9

They didn't get back to the city until the next evening. Neither one of them seemed to be in a hurry to return to normal life. They lingered over breakfast. They walked through the little village near the resort. They both bought Christmas presents for their families. It was a good day, an amazing weekend, probably the best one she had ever had with a man and she didn't want it to end. He had tried to rationalize how quickly things were moving for them, but she was still afraid of feeling so much for him. Afraid that this couldn't be so good, that it wouldn't last, because for her it seemed that every good thing in her life came to an end.

She opened the door of her apartment and he followed her inside, carrying some of her bags.

He placed them on the floor and then turned to face her. Asa Andersen was a swoon-worthy man and her heart never failed to beat a little faster whenever she looked at him. She had been with him for the past thirty-six hours and she still felt that rush of excitement. Her lips wanted to curl into a smile. She didn't want to be that woman who fell too fast and too hard. She knew she had to protect her heart, but it was hard, because he kept doing things that made her want to give it away.

"Thank you for this weekend," she said to him. "I almost like the snow. Almost."

"Thank you for coming with me." He grabbed her hips and pulled her into his hard body. Vivid images of the night before flashed in her mind. How amazing his hard, naked body looked. She had never been a fan of muscled men before, but Asa's body was a work of art, like a statue, covered in warm deep brown skin.

And the way he touched her... No part of her had gone unstroked or unkissed last night. He had been all about her pleasure and she had lost count of how many times she'd climaxed last night. And they hadn't even had sex.

What they did last night felt more intimate. She felt closer, more connected to him.

"I'll make you fall in love with this state yet. Greatest place in the entire world."

"Says the man who was born and raised in New Jersey."

He grinned down at her, then cupped her face in his hands and kissed her. She knew he meant for it to be a soft, sweet kiss, but she grew aroused. He kissed her so thoroughly that it never failed to make her want more of him.

"Stay with me tonight, Asa."

He looked pained.

"It's okay if you don't. I can be a lot."

"No!" He slid his hands underneath her coat and sweater. "I want you so bad I could burst. It's just that I have to be at work at midnight."

"Midnight! Why didn't you tell me? We could have been home this morning."

"There was no reason to come home early. I wanted to spend the day with you. I've got time for a nap and shower." He kissed her again, but much shorter this time.

"I would stay, but for our first time I'm going to need all night."

She sighed heavily. "You should probably stop kissing me then."

"I don't want to but I will. I'm working twelve to eight for the next couple of days, but I want to see you. Will you have dinner with me before I go in?"

"Yes."

"And Wednesday will you go see *The Nutcracker* with me?"

"You want to see that?"

"You said you wanted to go to the ballet—I want to be the man who takes you."

"Are you sure you can't stay?" she ask as her lips sought his throat. "I'll be quick. I promise."

He took her mouth in a quick, hot kiss before he stepped completely away from her. "I need to take my time with you. I can't explain why, but it's important that I do."

"Go home. Right now." She was feeling emotional and a little raw. Her heart was too open at the moment. "I can't be held responsible for my actions if you don't."

He gave her a little smile. "I'll see you tomorrow." He paused and looked at her for a long moment and she wondered if it was anywhere near as hard for him to walk away as if was for her to see him go.

"Good night, Asa."

"Good night, Hallie."

He left her alone and she felt ridiculously close to tears. Parting really was such sweet sorrow.

Hallie was up early the next morning catching up on work emails and grading the papers her students had submitted to her by email. She was heading back to work tomorrow after a week off and while she genuinely missed her students, she was a little sad to go back. She had been in pain for a lot of the week, but it had been one of the best weeks of her life. And that was because of Asa. She knew that when she went back that things would change and she wouldn't be able to see him as much, which made her sad, but she knew that it was for the best. She was going home for the holidays soon, and not having her heart caught up while she was away was probably for the best. Her flight was all set. She had spoken to her cousin, Derek, last night after Asa had left. He had a ton of plans for her visit. Cookie decorating, and Christmas shopping, because they had gone together every year since they were twelve. Her grandmother and mother were planning a big dinner in her honor. They were all so excited to see her.

She knew it would be hard to leave home, but she knew it wouldn't be as easy to leave New York as she expected. She had thought about Asa more times than she would've liked to admit since he'd left her last night. She hated liking a man that much, because she always felt that he couldn't possibly like her as much as she did him. She never wanted to be in that position again—thinking that everything was fine and being blindsided by rejection. So as much as she wanted to see Asa, she was going to play it cool. Go out with him when he asked and try her hardest not to fall head over heels in love with him.

There was a knock at her door and she looked to the clock on her laptop to see it was half past eight. It couldn't be Asa. He'd told her that he would see her tonight for dinner, but when she got up and looked in the peephole she saw that it was him.

Her heart beat a little faster. She was still in her pajamas, her short curls were probably sticking up all over her head, but she knew it was silly to be self-conscious around him. He had seen her at her worst. And he had seen her naked last night, her face twisted in pleasure. In the full light. No blankets covering them. There was no hiding from him now.

She opened the door and he was standing there with two coffees in his hand and a brown paper bag. "You want to have breakfast with me?"

She grinned at him. He was one of those men that made you fall in love with him. "I would like that very much. Come in."

He looked tired, but so damn sexy in a sleepy way, if that was possible. "I got oatmeal with fruit, but I wasn't sure you would like that so I got you a sesame bagel with cream cheese, too. Because another great thing about this city is the bagels—they are the best in the world."

"I get it, Asa. New York is the best place that ever existed. I won't doubt it ever again."

She smiled at him, but he didn't smile back. He just took a step forward and kissed her. "I want you to be happy. That's all."

He didn't say happy here. Or happy with him. Just happy. She found it incredibly sweet. She grabbed his hand and led him to her couch where they settled in and started to eat. Being from a small island off the coast of Florida, she didn't eat much oatmeal, but it was good on this icy morning. The heat was barely coming up this morning and she was glad to be snuggled in to a warm man on this cold day.

"How was work today?" she asked him.

"Nonstop. And it wasn't even a Saturday."

"Tell me about it."

"Somebody was tweaked out on some illegal substance and had to be subdued and then sedated before we could take him to the hospital. There was a domestic dispute where a wife stabbed her husband with a large fork in his chest, and last but not least we responded to a bar fight. Broken glass in everyone."

"I'm sorry, sweetheart."

"Don't be." He put his oatmeal down and wrapped his arm around her as he rested his chin on her hair. "It's a part of my job."

"You're so tired. You should go to bed."

"I should, but I don't want to get up. I like it here."

"You could sleep here. My bed is pretty comfortable." She had liked sleeping with him the other night. She liked the way he smelled and how his heavy arm felt wrapped around her. She had missed it last night when she'd slept alone. One night with him and she was becoming addicted.

"Yes." He kissed her forehead and then stood up to strip off his shirt, shoes and his pants. He stood before her in just a pair of gray boxers. She found him delicious and that ache started to form between her legs again. "Come lie with me for a little while." He extended his hand and they walked the three feet to her bed.

That was the good thing about being in a tiny apartment with a gorgeous man. They were never very far from a bed.

They crawled under the down comforter and he pulled her to him and just held her close. That was all. His eyes were closed and his hand was stroking up and down her arm, but he didn't make a single move.

He was aroused. She could feel it against her leg, but he hadn't even tried to kiss her yet. She knew he was tired from working so hard all night, but his body told her that he wanted her and she was more than happy to oblige.

She leaned in and kissed his throat. He made a sound deep in his throat that spurred her on. She moved her lips over to his Adam's apple and down to the base of his neck.

He responded and she was feeling a little bolder so she placed her hand between his legs and rubbed him through his underwear. He hissed out a breath. "What are you doing to me, Hallie?"

"I'm asking you to make love to me. I know you're tired, but I enjoy slow, sleepy sex." She kissed his mouth. "Have you tried it? It's quite good."

His lips curled into a smile and he took her mouth in a long deep kiss. And she felt like she was falling again, which always made her feel heady and happy, a new rush every time. He curled his hand over her behind and pulled her even closer to him so that their bodies were lined up just right.

"I planned an entire evening for us. Dinner, then *The Nutcracker*, and then I was going to take you back to my place and seduce you. It was going to take all night, but I couldn't stay away from you long enough. I couldn't even make it twenty-four hours. The only thing that got me through last night's shift was the thought of seeing you today. I wanted it to be special, but now I just want you so damn bad I can't think straight."

She pressed her mouth to his briefly then let out a long sigh. "Fine. We'll do it your way."

"Not my way. If I had my way I would have had you in bed the night I moved in."

"Oh, really?"

"When I saw you this weird thing happened and all my senses went on alert. I remember it was really hot that day even though it was October and you were wearing a sundress. White with little pink flowers that looked like cherry blossoms. I thought you were a different kind of pretty than most New York women. I liked that about you."

She never imagined she could feel so close to someone. She placed one hand on his cheek and kissed him again as she slid her hand inside of his underwear. "We'll wait until Wednesday when you're all rested, but in the meanwhile I'm going to make you feel good."

"No." He rolled on his back and pulled her on top of him. "We're going to make each other feel good."

Two days later Asa was headed back to the station with his partner, Miguel. Their shift had been fairly quiet so far. One heart attack. A couple of slip-and-falls, which of course reminded him of Hallie. He had spent every ounce of his free time with her the last few days. He had napped most of that day in her bed after they had eaten breakfast. She had stayed in bed with him for a while, but spent her time grading papers, and catching up on things to prepare her for her return to work. He had slept like the dead for those hours, feeling comfortable in her place, liking that he knew when he woke up she would be there. They had dinner together before his shift. She had made him honey-glazed salmon with fresh green beans and brown rice. It was nice and when midnight came near and he had to leave for work, he didn't want to. That was new for him. He was usually the one putting space between him and whoever he was seeing. But not this time.

He wanted to see more of her. In fact he was counting down the hours till he clocked out so he could be with her again. There was little that was better than coming home to someone who was happy to see you and that was what he got with her. His apartment had just felt like an apartment, but when she was with him, wherever they were felt like home.

"What's going on with you?" Miguel asked. "You've been weird these past couple of days."

"Weird?" He looked over at him.

"Yeah, quiet, but not depressed or anything. Like you're thinking about something."

"You know that slip-and-fall we had last week in front of the school?"

"Yeah? You said she was your neighbor."

"She is. We're seeing each other."

Miguel gave him a sly grin. "I knew you had a thing for her."

"I've never been with anyone like her."

"You think it could be serious?"

"Too soon to tell," he said, knowing that a week was far too early to know anything for sure. Their attraction could burn out; whatever they were experiencing could fade. But his gut was telling him something different. He could see himself in it for the long haul with her. "I'm taking her out to dinner at Gotham's Grill and then to see *The Nutcracker* tonight."

"Oh, so you're in love with her?"

The question jolted Asa. "I didn't say that."

"You must be if you're planning to spend that much on one date. You're not getting out of Gotham's for less than two-fifty and that's if she orders cheaply. Is she one of those picky, pain-in-the-butt girls? The kind who won't give a man a chance till she sees what's in his bank account?"

"You've met her. You know she's not like that. She teaches high school English to inner-city kids."

Miguel nodded. "She's a tough little thing."

"She's from the South and she's missing her family and isn't having a great time in New York, and I want to show her that it's good here."

A call came over the radio then, ordering all rescue units to report to the tracks near the Hudson River and Asa felt dread completely wash over him.

A commuter train had derailed. There were already casualties.

Miguel hit the sirens and looked over at him. "You had better cancel your reservations. You're not taking that girl anywhere tonight."

Asa didn't need to call Hallie to tell her that their evening was off. The television was on in the teachers' lunch room and she saw the derailment on the news. There were passengers trapped. Dozens and dozens of people injured. It looked like a scene from a disaster movie. Hallie knew Asa was there assisting in the rescue efforts. And even though she knew that he hadn't been in the crash, her heart jumped into her throat as if he were.

She got up from the table, leaving her salad half-eaten as she went for her cell phone. There was a text message from him.

Emergency at work. Sorry about tonight.

It struck her then that she had gotten similar messages from Brent. He had canceled on her countless times. He always had an excuse. He always told her it was an emergency, that things were life and death.

It was real estate.

She'd sworn to herself that she would never be with a man who put his career before her again. But Asa was the sender of the message this time and it really was life or death.

She sent him a text back.

Tell me you're okay when you can. I'll be up when you get home.

"Hallie?" Meredith, another English teacher walked

into the office. "Are you okay? Do you know someone on that train?"

"My boy…" She stopped herself from saying *boyfriend.* What was Asa to her? Were they in a relationship? It had only been a little over a week—did she have the right to call him her boyfriend? What exactly were they doing together? It never occurred to her to ask him, to question it in his presence. She was too busy feeling good. "I'm seeing a man who is a first responder. He's on-scene. I was just checking to see if he was okay."

"Is he?"

"I don't know yet. I'm sure he is. He's just doing his job."

"My husband is a police officer. I know the feeling."

She hadn't known that about Meredith and now she felt silly that she hadn't. "This is a new relationship. Does it get better with time?"

"No. It doesn't. The more you love them, the more you'll worry."

"Oh, don't tell me that. I'm not sure I'll be able to carry on with my days."

"You'll manage." Meredith smiled softly. "My guy works crazy shifts sometimes, and leaves me alone on weekends and nights a lot of the time. If you're ever in the same position, we should commiserate. I know a place that does endless margaritas and quesadillas that will simultaneously make you love the world and hate yourself."

"That sounds like fun. I would like that." The knot in her stomach loosened slightly. It was nice to know that she didn't have to be alone if she didn't want to be, anymore.

Chapter 10

It was a little after eleven that night when Asa got home. He had been on the scene of the derailment for ten hours and at work for nearly sixteen that day. Exhaustion had set heavily into his bones, but he didn't think he could sleep. At least not with the images of the carnage flashing through his mind.

Hallie's door flew open as soon as he walked past it. She was still mostly dressed. Her feet and legs were bare, but she was still wearing the dress she must have worn to work that day.

"Were you just going to walk past my door?" She had been worried. It was etched deeply into her face.

"I was coming back." He was going to drop his bag and then go see her. He knew she had been worried. He just wanted to shake off some of today before he went to her. His tough day shouldn't bring her down.

"You don't have to come back. I'll come with you." She closed the door behind her and stepped out into the hallway. He knew he wasn't going to be good company tonight, but he couldn't turn her away. He didn't want to be alone tonight.

Nodding, he led her to his apartment. "Sit down," she ordered him once they got inside. She went to the refrigerator and opened the door. "You should eat something. I can order Chinese or make you grilled cheese and tomato soup. I have salmon left over at my place." She shook her head. "No one wants to eat salmon after a tough day. It doesn't scream comfort food."

"Hallie..."

"I could go to the bodega and get you a slice of chocolate cake."

"You're not leaving this apartment."

She looked at him helplessly. "I want to do something for you. Let me."

Those simple words lifted some of the heaviness off him. "Just come sit with me on the couch."

She nodded and did as he asked, snuggling into his side. He felt calmer as he wrapped his arm around her and buried his nose in her springy short curls.

"Are you sure you're not hungry?"

"No. Not right now. It's late. I don't want to keep you up all night."

"I was worried about you. All day. They kept playing the footage on the news. It looked terrible."

"It was terrible. There were kids there. You think you're prepared for everything, but you're never prepared for that."

"Is everyone out?"

"Yes. People were only trapped in a couple of the cars."

"Did everyone make it?"

"No," he said simply, not wanting to go into detail. She didn't ask anything else and he was glad for that. He didn't really want to talk about it right now. "I'm sorry about tonight."

"Don't apologize. I'm happy you're home."

He kissed her forehead, glad she was here. It would be nice to come home to this every night. He was starting to understand his best friend, Marcus, who only seemed happy when he was home with his wife.

"Can I stay here tonight?"

"You don't need to ask."

"You shouldn't be so relaxed about that policy. I could be one of those clingy women who stay one night and never leave. I could be a complete and total nut job. You really don't know me that well."

He took her face in his hands and kissed her. "I know you well enough to know that I don't want you to leave."

"Let me run back to my apartment and lock up."

He nodded and she left him alone. He closed his eyes and tipped his head back to rest on the couch. He didn't have one clear thought. Just a bunch of images of the day flashing through his mind. He had been feeling a little weary lately. First the crane collapse and then this. When he had first started his job, he'd loved every single moment of it—the excitement of racing to the scene, the rush of using his medical training to save lives. These past couple of months he had lost the exhilaration he had felt before. He was starting to feel like maybe something huge was missing. He was wondering if he might have taken the wrong path in his life.

He felt movement at his feet and saw that Hallie was kneeling on the floor and removing his shoes.

He hadn't heard her return, but realized that she must have been back for a while. The Christmas tree was plugged in. The lights were dimmed. There was a beer on the coffee table before him.

"Asa?" She ran her thumbs over the top of his foot. "Is your job often like this?"

"Like what?"

"So devastating?"

"I wouldn't have gotten to know you if it weren't for my job."

She smiled up at him. "Talk about your silver linings."

"Come here." He reached for her hand and pulled her up on the couch.

She wrapped her arms around his middle as she rested her head on his chest. "I want to take care of you tonight."

"Just be here. That's all I need."

He lightly ran his fingertips across the exposed skin at the opening of her dress. Her skin was so soft, felt so good beneath his fingertips that he was content just to touch her there, but she let out a soft sigh and pushed herself closer to him and it made him want to feel more of her. His fingers grazed the fabric of her dress before his hand slipped inside of it. She wore no bra beneath it. There was nothing impeding his access to her breast, to her nipple, which he gently stroked. His intention wasn't to arouse her, or to turn this comfortable situation sexual. But he knew he was turning her on. He felt her nipple tighten. He felt her body go laxer. He cupped her breast, loving the way the weight felt in his hand. Loving that he was the only one getting to touch her so intimately.

She pulled away from him for a moment and pulled a condom out of her dress and handed it to him. "Hold this for me."

She unwrapped her dress then to reveal that she was naked beneath. "I wanted to wear something special for you tonight, but this was the best I could come up with."

He swallowed hard as he gazed at her body. Beautiful brown skin and curves. She had a birthmark on her hip, a scar on the lower part of her tummy. She was the sexiest woman that he had ever seen.

She straddled him and he felt the heat from her sex

through his pants. He wanted to burst from them, rip them off and toss them away, but he just watched her. She took the condom from his hand and undid his pants. There was a moment when she looked into his eyes and he felt like he could see the world in them, his future in them. But then her eyes went down to his manhood, which was fully erect. She stroked him, causing him to lose focus. "Do you want to do this tonight?"

He couldn't form words, he was so choked with lust and a dozen other emotions, so he just nodded. She opened the condom with her teeth and then rolled it down his length. He was expecting her to take his hand and lead him to his bedroom to start things, but she didn't. She rose up, took him in her hand and slid down onto him. There was no foreplay. No buildup. She was ready for him and let out a slow, deep moan as he filled her.

It was probably one of the most erotic moments of his life. He wasn't sure if it was that she was naked and pressed against his fully clothed body, or if it was because he had wanted this for so long, but it was wonderfully good. She kissed his mouth once before she started to move. Slow, long strokes. His hands sunk into the flesh of her behind and he watched her face. He wanted to close his eyes and give in to the sensation of being with her, but he couldn't look away. Her mouth was slightly open, her eyes closed, her breasts bouncing as she moved on top of him.

She dug her fingers in his shoulders as she rode, moaning and panting, calling out his name. He had her, but seeing her enjoy sex like this made him want her even more.

"Kiss me," he ordered as he cupped the back of her neck and pulled her mouth to his. Her pace quickened. He could feel her clenching around him and then her body went tight before the waves of orgasm shook her.

She wrapped her arms around him, burying her face

in his neck as she recovered. He was still hard inside of her, but he just held on to her, stroking his hand down her back, enjoying the feeling of having a satisfied woman wrapped around him.

"I'm sorry, honey."

"Why are you sorry?"

She kissed the seam of his throat. "I wanted that to be good for you."

"Do you think we're done yet?"

"I just wanted it to last longer. I've never orgasmed so quickly in my life." She kissed the side of his face, dropping slow pecks along his cheek. "I'm sorry." She kissed his shoulder. "But this is all your fault. If you weren't you, this wouldn't have happened."

I love you.

The thought rang out clearly in his mind. He had never been in love before, but he was in love with her, and he knew it with every fiber of his being. He couldn't tell her that yet because it was too soon and it was too crazy to fall in love so fast.

He rolled her onto her back and peeled off his shirt. "What's that supposed to mean?" He took her mouth in a hot kiss. Their chests were pressed together, no more barriers between them. He could feel her heart pounding.

"You do something to me. You touch me and the air goes out of my lungs. You kiss me and my thoughts fade away. I just want to be with you."

He pushed inside of her, starting their lovemaking all over again. "You will." After tonight he couldn't imagine himself letting her go.

Asa was off the next day, his body still sore from yesterday's rescue efforts, but he felt good, too. Relaxed. Calmer than he had in a long time. He lay on his couch for hours. The television was on but he couldn't focus on what was playing. He was thinking about his job and about Hallie and what had gone down between them last night. He kept reaching for her and she kept letting him have her, making love with him each time with the same intense passion that people talked about, which he'd never thought was real. He hadn't wanted to let her go this morning, but he did because she had to go to work, although they had lingered. He watched her get dressed. He made her stay for an extra cup of coffee. He kissed her goodbye about ten times before she actually got out the door.

His phone rang and he was forced out of his thoughts.

"Hello?"

"Brother!"

"My twin." He smiled, hearing his sister Virginia's voice on the phone. "I haven't heard from you in a month of Sundays."

"I've been working."

"Painting or interior design?"

"Both. Mostly painting, though. That portrait I did of Carlos when he returned for his first game after his injury got a lot of press. I've been contacted by a ton of athletes. I've turned most of them down, but I am going to do Rocky Afatia's."

"That huge Samoan football player with all the tattoos?"

"Yes. I think he is quite beautiful. I'm going to do a nude."

"Excuse me?"

"You heard me. He doesn't have a typical athlete's body. But he's just as powerful and as fast as a man half his size. Don't worry. It will be beautiful. I'm going to paint his wife, too. She is over six feet tall and has this amazing thick black hair that comes down past her butt. My fingers are itching to get to work." Asa heard the longing in his sister's voice. Their parents had been so against Virginia pursuing her painting career, but it was in her blood. She had always been a little different from the rest of them, a dreamer and an idealist, more adventurous than he could ever be. It was funny that she had married a man who had followed every rule and was probably the most grounded man he had ever met. But it was his unwavering support that had helped her pick up a paintbrush again after years of not painting and now she was more successful than ever.

"How have you been otherwise?"

"Good. Great, actually. I love having my husband home and I'm excited to see you for Christmas. I miss you."

"You could call me more often."

"You could call *me* more often," she countered. "I heard about the train derailment. Were you there?"

"Yes. We were one of the first units on the scene."

"Was it as awful as it looked?"

"It was worse, Gin. I don't ever want to respond to something like that again." But he knew it would happen again, because that was just the nature of his job. And for the first time he was seriously doubting if he wanted to continue there.

"How are you holding up?"

"I'm fine. Don't worry about me."

"I guess I don't have to anymore. Mom says that you are seeing someone."

"Did she?"

"She says that she really likes her, which is even more shocking. Mom doesn't like anyone. It took a while for Carlos to win her over and he's a gorgeous, beloved baseball player."

"Don't take it too hard. I'm just better at life than you."

She laughed. "I was so happy when you dropped out of med school. I thought they were really going to lay into you, but then you spring this knee brace thing on me and tell me you're financially set for life and it really put a damper on my happiness."

"I did it just to spite you, you know."

"Story of your life. So it's true, you have a girlfriend?"

They hadn't labeled it yet, but it felt right. Neither one of them was dating anyone else. "I'm seeing someone."

"Why are you so closemouthed about it?"

"I'm not. I'm sure Mom gave you all the pertinent information. Her name is Hallie. Her favorite color is purple and she really likes chocolate cupcakes."

"Who doesn't like chocolate cupcakes? I'll find out more about her when you come down. There won't be room at the house when you come."

"You mean to tell me in your enormous estate you don't have any spare space?

"Both sides of the family are coming down. Carlos's nieces and nephews, his mother and aunts. Our parents. We rented you a little house near the beach in town. It's a bit of a drive, but I figured you'd rather have your own space and some privacy. The house will literally be insane. Carlos's brother and sister also are staying in town."

"It's okay, Gin. You don't have to explain."

"I do, because you are the closest person to me on the planet and I feel bad, but I'm going to take you to lunch when you get here. Carlos wants to come, too, but I told him to get his own twin."

"It's okay if your husband comes. Carlos has become one of my best friends."

"I know. You text him more than you text me."

"You're a smelly girl."

"And you're a big jerk, but I love you."

"I love you, too."

"I'll see you soon. I'm so happy we'll be spending Christmas together."

Chapter 11

Hallie lay across Asa's bed, still trying to catch her breath, her underwear hanging off her ankle. There just hadn't been time to totally remove them. Asa had pulled her into a kiss as soon as she walked through the door and the next thing she knew they were pulling their clothes off and making frenzied love on top of his gray comforter.

"We were supposed to be going out to dinner," she said to him.

He grabbed her hand and laced his fingers through hers. "We can still go."

"No… I don't think I can walk. You've broken me."

He rolled over on to his side and grinned down at her. "You don't look broken to me." He kissed her shoulder as he smoothed his hand up her torso. "You look pretty damn amazing to me."

"Oh, don't look so proud of yourself."

"Did I get carried away? I missed you. I can't seem to control myself."

"You're every woman's biggest nightmare. You're fantastic in bed. You want to spend time with me and you say the nicest things. You're just terrible, Asa." She lifted her head and kissed him. "You didn't get carried away. I was there right along with you."

It was mid-December, three weeks into their relationship, and it still felt unreal to her. She slept with him every night that he was home. When she got off work she went straight to his apartment, bypassing hers because sleeping without him by her side just didn't seem right anymore. Whatever they had was intense and almost all-consuming. She was thirty years old. She didn't think this kind of hot and heavy fireworks existed, but she couldn't be near Asa without touching him and she was afraid that it was becoming too much. She had tried to put a little space between them, return back to her apartment at night, sleep alone. Give them both time to think, but Asa wouldn't allow that. There were days he worked double shifts and overnights, when it was impossible for them to be with each other. She missed him then, like she was missing a piece of her body. When he was home he was with her and she loved every moment of it, but they were moving so fast.

Things had started off well with Brent, too. There was a time when she had been really happy, when he wanted to spend a lot of time with her. She'd been so in love she hadn't seen the signs that had been there early on.

She wasn't sure what Asa was thinking. Whether he saw them as something that could get serious or if this was a little short-term fun for him. She was afraid to ask him. Afraid to bring it up because she didn't know if she wanted to hear the answer.

"I'm leaving to go home soon."

"Sleep here tonight," he said, kissing down her throat. "I was dealing with alcohol poisoning when I wanted to be in this bed with you."

"I am sleeping here tonight. You still have to feed me

dinner. I meant I was going home for Christmas. I'll be gone three weeks."

"I know," he said softly. "I've put it out of my mind."

"You'll be with your family, too."

"I know. My brother-in-law called me just before you walked in. He bought a boat. We're taking it out."

"Do either of you know how to drive a boat?"

"Of course not. But we're men. We'll figure it out or die trying."

He made her laugh. "You're going to have fun."

"I think so."

"You're going to be busy."

"My family takes up some time. But I'll remember to call you. We can FaceTime."

"Maybe you shouldn't call me those three weeks."

"Why?" He stiffened, his brow collapsing into a frown.

She shook her head, not sure how to put her feelings into words. But she was falling in love with him so fast she was afraid that when what she felt finally hit the ground the crash would devastate her. "What are we? What is this that we're doing?"

"We're together. You know that. This is not just one-sided. I know you feel the same way I do."

"I know, and that's what scares me. What if this is just passion? What if we are letting good sex cloud our judgment?"

"This is more than just good sex and you know it." He rolled onto his back. "Are you saying you don't want to do this anymore?"

"No. I'm saying that I think this is moving fast and I'm feeling things I'm not so sure I should be feeling after three weeks."

"Why are you so focused on time? Let yourself feel what you're feeling. Just be in the moment."

"And what happens when this moment ends? It's been eight months since I broke up with the man I spent the last five years. The man I thought I was going to marry."

"You're still in love with your ex," he accused.

"I'm not." She meant that. "You don't deserve to be my rebound and I don't deserve to be your Christmas fling."

"Why do you seem so sure of that? You have no clue what's going on inside of my head."

"I know, but I don't know what's going on in my head, either, and I can't think because all of my thoughts are about how I feel when I'm with you. I'm not saying I want to end this. I just think we both need time away from each other to think. To see if this holds up when we're not with each other."

"I think you're being ridiculous. If I call you once a week while you're away, it's not going to make a difference."

"I don't want to be that girl who is waiting for a phone call the whole week."

He climbed on top of her, settling his naked body between her legs. Her arousal spiked again. Not a slow burn, but a hot, quickly spreading fire. "You're still trying not to fall in love with me," he said.

"Yes."

He cupped her face in his hands and gave her a very slow, very deep kiss. She nearly melted into a puddle. "Stop trying," he whispered.

"You would like that, wouldn't you?"

He nodded just before he kissed down her throat. "A man likes to think he's lovable."

"Of course you're lovable. Why do you think I'm trying to slow this down?"

"Just stop." He kissed his way down to her chest.

"I can't end up with another broken heart."

He paused and looked down at her. There was an intensity in his eyes that scared her. "I'm not him. I'm not going to hurt you."

For some crazy reason she believed Asa wouldn't hurt her. Or he wouldn't mean to. She had thought that Brent could never hurt her the way he did, either. But Asa wasn't Brent. Nothing like him. He was decent to his core and treated her better than anyone ever had and that was why it was scary. She couldn't let herself trust anything this good. Because she knew how bad it would be if it went wrong.

"Damn you, Asa." Emotion pricked the back of her eyes and shut them.

"I just want to make you happy." His lips grazed her cheek.

"Don't call me when I leave. Let me be the one who calls you."

He sighed. "Fine. I don't agree, but I'll do this for you."

"Thank you." She opened her eyes and looked up at him again. "Now make love to me again. I really want a reason to miss you while I'm gone."

A few days later Hallie landed in Miami. She had thought she would feel elated as she walked through the airport toward the baggage claim where her cousin was waiting for her. But she didn't feel anything near that. It was as if something was missing, like she had left something important behind. She tried to shake off the feeling as she continued on alone. She was finally where she had been dreaming about for months. Flying into Miami was a different experience than flying into New York. The women here were wearing brightly colored sundresses and jump suits. Hair was in beachy waves and loose curls. Men sported white pants and candy-colored blazers. The pace here seemed slower, more relaxed, almost happier. It was the opposite of New York with all those people rushing around, their every move so important.

She had grown up here. She had longed for this environment, for these sights. She should be drinking them all in and enjoying every moment, but she realized that she was missing Asa. She'd slept alone, away from him last night in her own place, which wasn't something she had done in weeks unless he had to work. She had an early flight and had told him she needed to get to sleep early, which was true. But she couldn't sleep at all. She missed his heavy arm wrapped around her. She missed his warmth, the feeling of safety she had next to him.

She'd told him that she needed this time to clear her head, to detox from him. Detox was the right word. She had become addicted to being with him. And just when she'd convinced herself that the space was for the best he'd surprised her at the front door this morning with a cup of coffee and a long kiss goodbye.

Tears had splashed down onto her cheeks and she knew she was being foolish. She knew she shouldn't be reacting that way to a man she had known for less than a month. Especially when going home to Hideaway Island, the only place she had wanted to be since she'd left.

"Call me when you get there," he said with his lips still pressed to hers. "I'll see you when you get back."

Her mind stayed on that memory all throughout the day. She would see him when she got back. A few weeks ago she had made up her mind that once she came here she would never go back, but now…now that was no longer a certainty.

"Is that my baby?" Hallie heard her mother's voice and she was shocked to see her standing there with a bouquet of the wild lilies that grew on their island.

"Mom?" She ran to her, closing the distance between

them in seconds. Her mother wasn't supposed to be there, just her cousin. But her mother was there and as soon as Hallie felt her arms close around her, she felt the tears well in her eyes again.

"Oh, sweetheart. I've missed you so much."

"What are you doing here? I didn't know you were coming."

"We wanted to surprise you," Derek said. She looked up to see her handsome cousin and his mother there. She smiled when she saw him. She was so used to seeing him in paint-stained clothes and smelling slightly of wood and varnish, but he was wearing unstained jeans and a blue polo shirt. He had dressed up for the event.

"I'm so glad you did." She hugged him, too, and he lifted her up and spun her around in a big bear hug.

"Stop crying, you water head."

"I don't think I can." She pulled away from him and looked at her aunt Helena. "How are you, Auntie Lena? I've missed you, too."

"You'd better have. How's your head? We heard you did some damage to it."

"It's hard as a rock. I'm fine."

"Don't hog my baby." Her mother tugged her away from her aunt and hugged her again. "You look so pretty, Hallie. I wasn't sure if I would like your hair short, but I do. And your skin is gorgeous. You're glowing. I thought New York would wash you out."

"New York isn't bad. I can see why Daddy loved it there."

"But not as much as he loved Hideaway Island. Moving to the island was the best decision he ever made and I think—"

"Aunt Clara..." Derek warned. "Let's get Hallie's bags

and then take her out for lunch. I'm sure she's tired after her long flight."

"I am tired. Mom, could you please get me some coffee from that stand over there, while I get my bags. I was so excited I barely slept at all."

"Of course! Come on, Helena, let's see if they have any Cuban coffee there."

They watched their mothers walk off and Hallie looked up at Derek, an unspoken question passing between them.

"She's planning an all-out attack to get you to move back here for good. There will be lots of guilt. Some crying and probably a few threats thrown in there."

She nodded. "I expected as much."

"The worst part is that she's going to try to get you and Brent back together."

Hallie rested her head on Derek's arm. "Please tell me you tried to talk her out of it?"

"You know I still think we should string that punk up by his toes. Of course I've tried to talk her out of it and I will run interference when I can, but I can't stop her all the time."

"I know. I can handle it. Getting back with Brent is the last thing I want right now."

Chapter 12

A week later Asa departed from the ferry that brought him from Miami to Hideaway Island. He saw his brother-in-law and sister waiting for him at the end of the long ramp and while he was really happy to see them and be out of the freezing cold city, he knew he was missing Hallie. He respected her wishes and hadn't called her. He thought she might be trying to break things off and if that was the case, he wouldn't try to convince someone who didn't want to be with him to stay, but that wasn't the case with her. She wanted to be with him. He felt it with every glance and every kiss. He felt it in his bones. She was scared they were falling in love too fast. And she might have a point.

That was the only reason he respected her wishes. But she had called him the night she'd landed. And she texted him every evening. They had been apart for just about a week and he wondered if this little experiment was having the desired effect.

He didn't just miss the physical side of their relationship, he missed hearing her voice and sharing meals together, he missed hearing about her day. He missed coming home to her. She wasn't a fling. He loved her. But he wouldn't tell her that. Not when he was so unsure of how things would end up. Her ex wanted her back, and even though she told Asa she wasn't in love with him, a shared history could be too strong a bond to break.

"Asa!" His sister extended her arms. She was in one of those long, flowy, brightly colored dresses that she lived in. Her cheeks were round, maybe a little fuller than the last time he had seen her.

"Hey, twin." He gave her a tight hug. "When were you going to tell me that you were pregnant?"

"What?" she and her husband Carlos said at the same moment.

"How are you, Carlos?" He nodded at her brother-in-law briefly before he looked back to Virginia. "What are you, about nine weeks?"

"How do you know?" Virginia ran her hand over her stomach. "Am I showing?" she whipped around to look at her husband. "You told me I wasn't showing!"

"You're not!"

"A medical professional knows these things."

"That's crap and you know it."

"I honestly don't know how I knew. I just knew the moment I hugged you."

"You two have some kind of freaky twin thing going on." Carlos shook his head. "I'm surprised that you don't cry when she's in pain."

"Of course I don't cry when she's in pain. We're not identical," Asa said. "You're not having twins, right?"

"No! I'm not sure I could handle that right now. We're going to announce it at our big Christmas party."

"So you were going to make me wait and find out with the rest of the world? I've been with you since the moment you were born. We shared a womb and a crib for the better part of a year. I know you better than anyone else on the planet and could argue that you should have told me the moment you found out."

"I'm her husband," Carlos protested. "She wasn't going to tell you before she told me."

"Husbands are replaceable, man. Twin brothers are forever."

Virginia looked at Carlos and shrugged. "I think Asa gets to find out first the next time we get pregnant. It's only fair."

"Are you serious?"

"Nah." Asa slapped Carlos on the back. "We're busting your chops, but you shouldn't keep things from me."

"I won't." Virginia nodded. "I'm actually glad you know. I'm having a hard enough time keeping the secret from Mom. She's been walking around the house commenting on which rooms would make a good nursery."

"You think she knows?"

"No. She told Carlos that he was getting older and that it was time he stopped messing around and made them grandparents."

"She's doesn't tiptoe around things, does she?"

"No." Virginia looped her arm through his. "We're going to show you to your place and then take you to lunch. I think you'll like staying there. We might stay with you, just to get away from all the fuss at our house."

"I thought elderly people were supposed to be forgetful and not as quick as they were in their younger days," Hallie said to her eighty-two-year-old grandmother as she sat across from her at the kitchen table. "I think you've gotten a little quicker in your old age. In fact I think you've become a card shark. How have you beat me five times in a row?"

"It's very simple, dear. I'm a genius and you aren't yet."

"Nanny!"

"What? I said you aren't a genius *yet*. It'll come to you."

Hallie laughed. "I've missed you, Nanny."

Nanny reached across the table and took her hand. "I've missed you, too. I'm glad you're home. This place hasn't been the same without you."

"I'm sure it's not so different."

"It is. You know I'm getting older. I don't have so many years left."

"Did my mother put you up to guilting me?" Hallie raised a brow at the elderly woman who didn't look more than sixty. "Your mother lived to be one hundred and six. Her mother lived to ninety-nine. You work out every day and you're in better shape than I am. Don't play the limited-time-left card with me."

"I'm busted." Nanny grinned. "But I do miss you and I do want great-grandbabies. You and Derek need to get to it."

"But there are more cousins."

"They aren't ready yet. You two are the eldest. Time to get your lives going."

"But..."

"No buts." Nanny stood up and crossed the table to pinch her cheek. "Do what Nanny says and the world will be a better place."

Hallie shook her head and watched as her grandmother left the room. She always got the last word. Hallie knew it would be foolish to say anything else.

Her mother walked into the kitchen, stopping to kiss her forehead before she went to the refrigerator. "I'm going to make some sandwiches from the leftover roast chicken from last night. Can I make you one?"

"Oh, no thank you. I'm going out with Derek. It was

the only free day he had. Between his furniture business and being mayor, he has no free time at all."

"And no time for a girlfriend. I tell him every night when he shows up for dinner."

"I can't believe he still comes over every night for dinner."

"Of course he does. I'm a way better cook than his mother and everyone knows it. Plus Nanny lives here, too, and Derek would rather have great food in a beautiful warm home with people he loves, than eat takeout alone. Plus, it gives me someone else to mother. It's a win-win."

"Speaking of mothering, you've been outdoing yourself since I've been here. You've cooked gourmet-quality meals twice a day. You've made my bed while I was still practically in it and you anticipate my every want and need before I even know I want or need it. I appreciate you, Mom, but you don't have to do so much. I'm happy to be here."

"Are you?" She walked away from the refrigerator and took the seat besides Hallie. "I feel like there is something off with you. You seem a little sad."

"Do I?" She was having so much fun being home with her family. Being back here soothed a raw part of her soul, but she still felt a little empty. Not speaking to Asa hadn't helped her clear her mind at all.

Maybe it was because she texted him every night. But she knew that wasn't it. Not seeing him or hearing his voice wasn't slowing down her feelings. Being back home didn't magically make her forget about him. She really missed him so much it hurt.

"Is it because of Brent? Does being back home remind you of all the good times you had here?"

"Um, no. I'm fine, Mom."

"You're not. Have you seen Brent? I was sure he would have stopped by. He asked about you a hundred times since you left. Must be out of town. He spends a lot of time at his

Miami office. He has a sixty-seven-million-dollar listing. He showed me pictures of it on the internet, and I nearly passed out in my chair. I thought Carlos Bradley had a nice house, but there is a museum in that house. They could charge admission."

"It can't be as nice as Daddy's work."

"No." Her mother sobered and smiled softly. "Your father would have hated it, thought it was disgustingly garish with no charm. He would have said 'Nobody needs to live in a house that damn big. It's wasteful. Money and class are two things that don't necessarily go together,'" she imitated her late husband's voice. "That man of mine."

"I miss Daddy," Hallie whispered, feeling the pain sneak up on her. He had passed away last year just before the holidays and they'd had a very low-key Christmas without him. It wasn't Brent that was making her feel funky, and she knew it had to be more than Asa. She was missing her father who had loved this holiday so much.

"Oh, honey. That's it, isn't it? You miss your father. It's hard being in this house without him."

She nodded. She could almost hear his footsteps, almost see him at his desk drinking coffee.

"I thought I would go nearly insane those first few months. I tried not to let it show, but I almost couldn't take being here, but memories of your father are here and I want to be here with them."

"He would hate it if you lived in a house he hadn't built."

"There's one for sale in town. They are charging a fortune for it, too. Your father would have hated that."

"Yes, but he was the legendary Hal Roberts. People will pay to live in one of his masterpieces."

"He would never call them masterpieces. He would just say he was having fun. That's why I loved the man. My family didn't understand why I fell in love with a man over twenty years older than me, but I couldn't help myself. He was so dashing and brilliant and funny. He used to make me laugh until my cheeks and sides hurt. He made me feel so alive. Luckily they came around when they saw how happy he made me."

"I had the oldest dad in school, which some people thought might be a bad thing, but I knew I had the best dad."

"And to think we almost didn't get together."

"You didn't? I didn't know that."

"Your father thought I was too young for him. He thought people would think he was a dirty old man and he kept pushing me away. But we were equals. He treated me as his equal and he sought out my advice and he needed me just as much as I needed him. I knew I wasn't going to find that love in another twenty-two-year-old so I went after your father and I didn't stop until he admitted that he was meant for me and I was meant for him."

"That's so sweet. You were like his little stalker."

She laughed. "It's true. But if you really want something out of life, you have to go and get it."

Derek walked through the kitchen door then, her handsome cousin smiling down at both of them. "My favorite women." He kissed Clara's forehead. "I'm stealing your daughter for the day."

"Your annual cousin day." She nodded. "Bring me back a slice of key lime pie and stop at the grocery store on your way back and bring me two dozen eggs."

"Two dozen eggs?" Hallie shook her head. "We have a bunch in the refrigerator."

"You silly girl, it's Christmas time. We are baking cookies tomorrow. Some for us and the rest for the senior citizen home."

"Of course." Hallie laughed. "That should be fun. I'm looking forward to it."

* * *

Carlos and Virginia had rented Asa a cottage walking distance from the beach. He liked it, liked that he could see the ocean in the distance, but it didn't feel like Christmas there like it had in New York City. There hadn't been a single decoration in the house. If this were any other year he wouldn't have even noticed. He normally never decorated his apartment for Christmas, but he and Hallie had done so this year. Every night she plugged in the tree; she had even brought twinkling lights for the window. He would forever associate Christmas with Hallie, and the fact that it looked and felt like summer in his temporary island home just reminded him that he was going to spend the holiday without her.

"What's the matter, Asa?" Virginia asked as they walked into the elegant but understated waterfront restaurant.

"Nothing. I'm just tired."

"Did you work last night?"

"I was supposed to work a three-eleven, but I got off late. There was a bad car accident in Midtown and the rescue unit got called in."

"Do I want to hear how that story ends?"

"No."

The hostess recognized Carlos right away and seated them at a table that overlooked the marina in the quieter part of the restaurant. There were a few perks to having a brother-in-law that was a baseball legend.

"I'm not sure I could handle your job. You deal with tragedy every single day."

"It's not all bad." No, not all bad, but it had been getting harder and harder to do. The crazy hours, the physical toll on his body. It was becoming incredibly difficult to shake off what he was seeing as time passed. He rarely saw people at their best, more often seeing the humanity at their worst moments.

"Do you think you'll stay with this job until retirement?" Carlos asked him.

If anyone had asked him that last year his answer would have been a resounding yes, but as the days went by…he wasn't so sure that he would.

His sister was pregnant and that brought the idea of having a family to the forefront of his mind. He worked crazy shifts. He didn't want to miss his kid's games or parent-teacher conferences because he was stuck at work.

"I don't know," he answered honestly.

"You have options."

"Finish my internship and residency? I want to work less hours, not more."

Carlos nodded. "I know. My little brother, Elias, is busting his butt to finish his surgical residency. We rarely see him, but that's not what I was talking about."

"What are you talking about?" he asked him.

"Yeah," Virginia said. "What are you talking about?"

A woman walking by caught Asa's attention. She was wearing a sweet pink-and-white sundress, her hair in short curls.

It was impossible for her to be here. It probably wasn't Hallie, just some woman who resembled her, his missing her causing his mind to go crazy. But he reached out anyway, and grabbed the woman's wrist. He was unable to stop himself. It was the way she held herself, the way her hips swayed. It was the dress she wore. The flowers looked like cherry blossoms and he would know it anywhere because that was what she'd worn when he had first laid eyes on her the day he moved in.

He pulled her into his lap. Her eyes went wide and she smiled beautifully at him as recognition dawned on her.

"Asa."

He wasn't sure who moved first but they were kissing each other. Her hands on his face. His arms wrapped tightly around her.

How could she be there, right on the day he had been thinking about her the most?

"I'm so glad you don't listen," she said when she broke the kiss, but her lips didn't go far. She kissed him all over his cheeks.

"I listened to you. I'm not here to see you." He closed his eyes and let himself be kissed. If it were any other woman he would have hated this treatment, but he liked it with her. This was what he had been missing all week, "I told you your idea was dumb."

She smacked his shoulder. "Now is not the time to tell me 'I told you so.' What do you mean you're not here to see me?"

"This is where my sister and her husband live."

"Hi!" Virginia said, and Asa remembered that they weren't alone. The whole world kind of melted away when they were together, but they were in the middle of a restaurant on the busiest part of the island.

Hallie's head snapped up. "You're Carlos Bradley's wife."

"Well, I'd like to think I'm more than that, but it's true. I am married to the hottie."

"Hello." Carlos waved. Both he and Virginia were grinning.

"Oh, boy. I think this is one of those moments when you want to curl up in a ball and die."

"I take it you know this guy?" She heard Derek's voice but was afraid to look up at him. She didn't want to look at anyone except Asa. She couldn't believe that she was meeting Asa's sister this way. She couldn't believe she hadn't noticed Asa's twin and her legendary baseball player husband sitting there. "I saw him pull you into his lap and was about to kill him."

"Is this your ex?" Asa's jaw clenched. He was primed for a fight and Hallie thought he looked sexy and terrifying at the same time.

"Of course not. This is my cousin."

"Oh, what's up, man? I'm Asa." Asa extended his hand. "It's nice to meet you. Hallie loves you. She talks about you all the time."

"Asa's my twin brother, Derek," Virginia spoke up. "Isn't it a small world?"

"Very small. I wish I had known about you, Asa. You seem to make my cousin very happy."

"You remember that paramedic neighbor I told you about? This is him." Hallie looked back up at Asa and fiddled with his collar. "I've grown very fond of him."

Asa gave her a soft smile and then kissed her again. Her eyes drifted shut again, even though this kiss was much shorter than the last one. She really had missed him. Being this close to him again made that hollow feeling she had been dragging around with her for the past week vanish without a trace. She hadn't wanted to fall in love with him, but she had lost that battle and the defeat had been brutal. "You've got to stop kissing me."

"Stop looking so embarrassed."

"I *am* embarrassed."

"It's just family here."

"That's exactly why I'm mortified. I never expected to meet your sister this way."

"But you did expect to meet my sister eventually." He had a smug look on his face and she wanted to smack him. Every night when she texted him, he told her to let him call. To FaceTime him.

There's no slowing this down.

"We can talk about that later." She tried to get up, but Asa wouldn't let her. His hand was just beneath the hem of her dress, clamped around her thigh. Not tight enough to hurt, but firmly enough to show possession. She grew slightly aroused. She tried to push the feeling away, because their families were watching them closely, but Asa had a look in his eye that promised hours of hot, mind-numbing bliss when he got her alone.

"Stay."

"Have you eaten yet?" Virginia asked. "We haven't ordered. Please stay. I would like to get to know you."

"I would feel awful. I know Asa hasn't seen you in months I don't want to intrude on your time together."

"If you go, we're just going to talk about you."

"If we go," Derek started, "I'm going to grill you about your boyfriend, so it might be better if we just have lunch with the Bradleys and get this over with."

"Stay, Hallie," Asa urged. "I missed you."

"Okay." She nodded. "But you have to let me sit in a chair and not in your lap."

"I reluctantly agree." That hot look was still in his eye and she wondered how long it would be before she could be alone with him.

Where could they be alone? He was probably staying with his family. She was staying with hers and she was pretty sure her mother wouldn't appreciate her sharing her childhood bedroom with a man she wasn't married to.

She stood up and looked at Derek, who didn't seem upset with her for keeping Asa a secret, just kind of bemused by it all. She had promised to spend the day with him. They had been planning this day for weeks and he was so busy. She couldn't desert him now. "We'll go Christmas shopping after this. I promise."

He nodded. "It's okay. I'm going to tell our waitress that we're moving over here, so she isn't confused."

"Good idea." Virginia stood. "Let's all move to that bigger table over there."

Asa grabbed her hand as he got up, stroking his thumb across her palm. "I hate that you look so unsure of yourself right now." He leaned in to speak quietly in her ear. "You've met my mother. My sister is a piece of cake."

"I wasn't your girlfriend then."

"Right now is the first time you're admitting that you are my girlfriend."

"I guess we'll talk about that later, too."

"When is later?"

"I don't know. You just got here. You'll probably be busy with your family."

He nodded. "I have to say my hellos. I have a house to myself, though. Come stay with me."

"I might have to sneak out at night."

"Do what you can."

"I was heading to the ladies' room when you yanked me into your lap. I still need to go there."

"Go. I'll save you a seat next to me."

Asa watched Hallie walk away. He was having a hard time pulling his eyes off her. He wasn't sure how it was possible that she'd grown even sexier since he had last seen her. Maybe it was that her skin was sun-kissed, making it a richer, deeper brown.

There was no denying that she had been excited to see him, that she missed him as much as he missed her. He couldn't wait to get her alone, to peel off every inch of her clothing and just kiss his way down her beautiful body.

He felt a hard slap on his arm and he looked down to

see Virginia fuming. "You told me you were seeing somebody. You never told me you were in love."

"You didn't tell me you were pregnant."

"That's different!"

"Yes, yours is a way bigger secret."

"Wait until I tell Mom."

"You tell her and I'll put spiders in your bed."

"Hey!" Carlos stepped between them. "I sleep in that bed. No spiders. And Gin, baby, you have to admit that you two are kind of even. I don't recall you rushing out to tell Asa the moment you fell in love with me."

"See? That's two things you've left me in the dark about."

"This is a bigger deal, Asa. You've never been in love before. I've met your girlfriends. You've never looked at any of them the way you look at her."

He didn't think it was that noticeable. "I'm crazy about her. Literally crazy about her."

"And Mom likes her, too." She reached into her bag and pulled out her planner.

"What are you doing?" he asked her.

"Checking my calendar. I've got to clear my schedule for your wedding."

Chapter 13

"I like Asa," Derek said to her as they walked through historic downtown Hideaway Island.

Hallie took a deep breath in as she nodded. There was something about this place that was magical. The salty ocean air, combined with the beautiful candy-colored shops that were nestled between the old Spanish-inspired buildings. And it had been transformed for Christmas. Not in the same classic way New York had been, but in a more whimsical way. The palm trees were decorated with garland and tinsel and a holiday display of Santa in a boat being pulled by dolphins was in the center of town. There were sandmen instead of snowmen. Christmas in New York was iconic, but Christmas by the beach felt like home to her. She wondered what Asa thought of it all. Or if he would miss not being in his beloved city for the holiday.

"When were you going to tell me about him? You've been home for a week."

Hallie looked over to her cousin after realizing that he was still speaking to her. She was distracted—by being back home, by Asa, by the long meal they had just shared with Virginia and Carlos.

"I wasn't sure what to tell you. It's still new. I feel like I've known him forever, but it's still so new."

"If he weren't Virginia's brother, I would have some major reservations."

"I know you made some pieces for their house a few years ago and Carlos Bradley secretly supports all your little charity projects around the island, but how well do you know them?"

"Pretty well. They are down-to-earth people. I've had a few dinners with them. They are the wealthiest citizens in our town. It's a mayor's job to kiss a little behind now and then. Plus I had a thing for Virginia for a long time."

"Excuse me?" Hallie stopped in her tracks. She and Derek were close, but they never talked much about their love lives, especially him. She just knew he had incredibly discreet relationships with women who were slightly older than him and who weren't looking for a commitment.

"Oh, yeah, before she and Carlos were a couple. She was his interior designer first and I went over to the house to introduce myself to him and there she was. I nearly forgot my name."

"What happened?"

"Isn't it obvious? Bradley took one look at me and knew what I was thinking. He made it incredibly clear that he was going after her and that I had better back down."

"It's not like you to back down. I saw you nearly take the head off that real estate investor guy who wanted to build that huge resort."

"That was different. He was trying to deface my town. I love this place more than anything on the planet. And I knew Virginia was already falling for Carlos when we met. I could see it in her eyes. Just like I see it in yours."

"Virginia and Asa are very close." She had never thought fraternal twins were as linked as identical twins, but Asa and Virginia were. They tilted their heads the same way when they thought about something. They finished each other's sentences and even ordered the exact same thing for lunch, right down to the dessert.

"I know. It was almost freaky watching them together. He's just the male version of her. Did you like her?"

"Of course I did. She's great. I'm just wondering what they thought of me. I felt so stupid today."

"Because you kissed your boyfriend in the middle of the restaurant like you hadn't seen him in a long time? Nobody is judging you for that. I think she likes you more because it's obvious how much you care for her brother. For what it's worth, you have my blessing."

"Blessing for what? It's way too soon for blessings. I'm crazy about Asa and I like my job in New York okay, but I miss this place, Derek. I might be happy with Asa, but I don't think I can be happy in New York for the rest of my life."

"Have you talked to Asa about this yet?"

"No. I'm not sure if there is anything to talk about. He's a rescue paramedic with the FDNY in the most exciting city in the world. He scales buildings and saves people from train crashes. He's a hero who loves his job and New York City. I couldn't ask him to move to a place where the most exciting thing that happens is Founder's Day."

"Hey, Founder's Day is amazing. There's fireworks and a parade. We roast a pig. It's one of the best things on the planet"

"Derek, you know what I mean. It's only been a little while, but what if he did it, what if he threw caution to the wind and moved back down here with me? Where would he work? Our fire department is volunteer. He would be bored here, and I would miss here too much if I stayed gone." She sighed. "I blame you. Your love for this island is infectious."

"It's hard not to be here and love it. But if it's meant to be, it will be."

"Would you move for a woman?"

"Are you crazy? I was born here and I'll die here." He took hold of her arm and pulled her into a little shop that sold soaps and fragrances. "We'll get Nanny's gift from here. You're going to go half on the gift basket with me. That gardenia soap alone is sixty bucks."

"I get my bodywash at the supermarket for less than five bucks and it lasts me five or six weeks. Our grandmother literally uses three dollars' worth of soap every morning."

"She told me that ladies must smell expensive and clean when I asked her why she used the same soap for sixty years."

"That is something she would say."

Derek walked away from her to talk to the shop owner about something that was troubling her. That's what he did as mayor. There were no days off for him. Whenever anyone had a problem, he listened. Hallie was used to it as his cousin, but she wasn't sure how many women could go through it as his wife.

She looked around the store for a few minutes, picking up little things here and there. There was a small soap set containing gently scented, beautifully wrapped bars. She immediately thought of Asa's mother. The small gift would be just right for the fierce but elegant woman.

And just as she was putting the package up to her nose for another sniff, a ghost from her past walked up to her.

He didn't look the same. He was a little thinner than before, no longer decked out from head to toe in exorbitantly priced designer duds. He almost looked like he had when they'd first starting dating five years ago. Only the boyishness was gone and left was a handsome but weary-looking man. "Hallie… How are you? You look incredible."

"No." She shook her head, no other word coming out. She was surprised that she was still so angry at him. There was no sadness there. No broken heart. It was anger. Anger she never got to express when she was with him last. She had been too hurt and stunned to say much to him when he broke up with her. "I have nothing to say to you."

His mouth dropped open slightly and for a moment, he looked like he didn't recognize her. Maybe he didn't. She had changed in the last eight months. Her identity was no longer wrapped up in being with him "I…"

"I don't think we need to talk," she said, keeping her voice quiet and calm. She wouldn't play the hysterical-woman role. She hadn't cried when he was breaking up with her, telling her that she wasn't good enough for him, and she certainly wasn't going to do it now. "I don't think we need to hash things out. You said everything you needed to say the last time we spoke. When you said it was over, it really was."

"Hallie, are you okay?" Derek was back. He stood closer, placing his hand on her shoulder in a protective brotherly move, as he looked at Brent.

"I'm fine. I think we're done here. Let's check out." She attempted to brush past him, but he grabbed her hand.

"Hallie. I was a complete and total jackass."

"Tell us something we don't know," Derek said.

Brent glared at him. The two men had never been big fans of each other. Derek thought he was too materialistic and Brent thought Derek was too much of a do-gooder. "I was talking to your cousin." He looked back to her. "I was wrong. I've missed you."

"I really don't care." She tugged her hand away from him and walked away.

"I'm not going to stop trying," he called after her.

She sighed. That was exactly what she was afraid of.

Asa's body felt heavy as he relaxed on the lounge chair on Virginia's back patio. It was getting late, a little before ten. He was exhausted after getting less than three hours of sleep this morning. But he was comfortable where he was for the moment. His mother and father were snuggled together on the love seat. Virginia and Carlos were half lying on the couch, their bodies stuck to each other like they were one person. They were as in love as two people could be.

Asa kept noticing Carlos's hand going to his wife's belly. They weren't going to be able to keep the secret for long. Asa couldn't have been the only one to have seen it. But maybe, even though there were twenty people scattered around the house and grounds, they hadn't.

Carlos's mother and sisters had gone for a moonlight walk along the beach. His brother-in-law was at the fire pit with his children roasting marshmallows. And the rest of them were just enjoying the quiet. Carlos and Virginia lived in an oceanfront mansion on the far side of Hideaway Island that had barely been developed. The only thing there was this house, surrounded by wild nature, which made it beautiful in a raw way. It seemed like one of the only places that the outside world couldn't infiltrate. He wasn't worried about the next big catastrophe, or trying to revive broken and mangled bodies. None of that could touch him here. He had never understood why his sister and her husband liked to hole up in this house that was so far away from the world, but sitting here tonight he did.

Being here with someone you were in love with must feel like paradise.

His phone rang then and he pulled it out of his pocket to

see that it was Hallie. He shook his head and smiled down at his phone. "Excuse me for a moment."

He walked back in the house, answering the phone as he did. "I almost thought you were going to stick to this no-talking thing while we were here."

"I should just to spite you," she said softly. "I wasn't sure you would still be up. I noticed how tired you were."

Of course she had noticed how tired he was. He had seen the slight bit of concern in her eyes at lunch when she looked at him. "I'm still at my sister's house. We had a late dinner."

"I got in not too long ago myself. I just finished shopping with Derek. Go back to your house and get some sleep. I just wanted to hear your voice before I went to bed."

"You think I'll be able to sleep knowing you're near? I've had a hard time sleeping without you this past week. My bed is not the same without you in it."

"Don't you try to charm me, mister. What will my mother think?" She let out a long sigh and he thought he heard some tiredness in her voice, but it was more than that. She sounded weary.

"What's the matter, baby?" Her cousin knew about them now. He wondered if she had said anything to her mother about today, about him, period. And what would she have told her if she did?

He'd felt her discomfort at lunch when Virginia was asking how long they had been dating. They had just made a month. And a week of that they had spent apart. How could they have been together and not have known where each other was going, Derek wanted to know. Hallie had flinched when he asked it and Asa knew what she had been thinking. They hadn't been together long enough. There was still a lot about each other that they didn't know yet. Or at least it seemed like that to the outside world and maybe they were right, but Asa didn't care what they thought. He just knew he was in love with the woman.

"Where are you staying?" Hallie asked him. "I think I need to see you tonight."

"Seacoast Avenue. House 117."

"I know that street well. How soon can you get there?"

"I left five minutes ago."

He disconnected, hearing her laughter as he did. He turned to head back outside, but saw his mother standing just inside the door.

"Unless you have a secret woman stashed on this island, I'm assuming Hallie is here."

They had said nothing to his parents when he first arrived. Carlos's aunts had arrived a few moments after he did. It was too happily chaotic to mention it then.

"She's from here."

"Why didn't you tell me this before?"

"I didn't know before today when I ran into her in town."

His mother raised one of her perfectly arched brows, showing a bit of displeasure. "You didn't know where she was from?"

"The name of the town never came up. And who would have thought here of all the places? This tiny island."

"It is quite the coincidence. I thought you told me she wasn't your girlfriend."

"She wasn't that day."

"And now you're in love with her?"

He nodded. There was no use in denying it.

"After a month?"

"After a month."

"I can't very well say anything to you, can I? Before

your sister got married, she fell in love with every poet and starving artist within a hundred miles."

"And she's moved across country for a few of them, too."

Dr. Andersen gave him a slight smile. "You think I've forgotten that? Hallie is a lovely girl. But if you didn't even have the time to find out her town, how could you know all the other important things about her?"

"Mom, I—"

She held up a hand, stopping his reply. "I'm just telling you to be cautious."

"I've never been happy playing it safe."

"No. Neither of my children are. I'm not sure where I went wrong." She smiled and gave him a little wink. "Go. You have someone waiting for you."

"Tell everyone goodbye for me."

"Will do," she said as he rushed through the house and toward his rental car.

Chapter 14

Hallie walked quietly toward her mother's bedroom, hoping her mother was asleep. She usually was in bed by nine thirty every night. Her mother had always joked that one of the benefits to having an older husband was getting to go to bed early. It wasn't true, though. Her father used to stay up late, sometimes all night if he was designing something. Even up to his final days he would make plans for fantasy structures, build models for them while his wife was slumbering.

Just as Hallie suspected, her mother was fast asleep. She was glad for that. She wouldn't have to give an explanation to her face or hear the inevitable questions that would follow. She stuck a note to her door that said that she was meeting a friend for a drinks and that she might be back very late.

"Where do you think you're going, young lady?" She heard from behind her.

She turned around to face her grandmother who was in a floor-length long-sleeved nightgown. Her white hair swept up elegantly.

"Hi, Nanny. Just going out to have a drink with a friend.

Don't wait up." She took a backward step toward freedom. "I'll have my cell phone on. Call if you need me."

She turned and tried to make a break for it.

"You're going to see a man, aren't you?"

Hallie let out a gasp. She couldn't even lie her way out of this one. Nanny would know. She walked closer to Nanny so that her sleeping mother wouldn't hear. "How did you know that?"

"I was listening at your door when you were on the phone."

"Nanny!"

"I may be old but my hearing is spectacular. Who is he? You haven't been home long enough to meet someone."

"He's my neighbor from New York. He lives down the hall from me and we have been seeing each other for a while. His twin sister is Virginia Bradley."

"Ah." Nanny nodded. "And you're in love with this boy?"

"What?"

"Dear girl, I know your hearing isn't bad. You heard what I said. You're in love with him. I heard it in your voice when you spoke to him."

"We're just dating. That's all." She had barely admitted to herself that she was in love with him—how could she admit it to anyone else? "I like him a great deal. A whole hell of a lot."

"But you're gun-shy. That Brent boy hangs out here more than he should, and certainly way too much for a man who broke our baby's heart. He makes it clear that he wants you back."

Hallie shook her head. Her mother had mentioned Brent showing her pictures of one of his listings. She should have figured he had come here to do it. "There's no going back. I can't go backward."

"No. It wouldn't be very productive, would it?"

"You don't think I should go back with him, do you?" She held her breath: her grandmother's opinion was very important to her.

"Please, child." She rolled her eyes. "I'd rather you die a spinster with nine cats than go back to that fool."

"I love you, Nanny." Hallie grinned at her grandmother. She really had missed her while she was in New York and she hadn't realized how much until she was with her again. It was infinitely nice to have someone older and wiser to turn to.

"I love you, too. Now go meet that man and have a good time."

"Don't tell Mom. I would like to tell her about Asa myself."

"Asa? It means healer." Nanny nodded approvingly. "Your heart needed a little healing. Your secret is safe with me."

Hallie gave her grandmother a quick hug and then rushed out of the house to meet Asa. Seacoast was one of the nicest streets in town. Not because it held large luxury homes, but because it had been perfectly planned. Lush landscaping, and unique architecture. Each house had a view of the ocean and the perfect orangy-purple sunsets that engulfed that island. It was in the middle of town, but it felt quiet and intimate and homey. It felt like Hideaway Island should feel, like it had been for the past hundred years.

She took her time walking up to Asa's house and the door swung open.

"You walked?" He looked annoyed.

"Yes. My car is in New York."

"You walked through town at night. Alone."

"It's fine. My parents' house is three blocks over. It's less than a ten-minute walk."

"Anything can happen in ten minutes." He grabbed her hand and pulled her inside.

"I grew up here. It's safe. It's so safe the cops are bored and have taken to helping the townsfolk with their housework during the days."

Asa shook his head, looking unconvinced.

"I walk alone at night in New York. It gets dark so early there in winter—it's dark before five."

"I don't like you alone then, either." He wrapped her in a hug and held her tightly to him. "I missed you."

He was never afraid to say it. He was never afraid to show affection anywhere. He never wanted or required her to act a certain way. She felt special with him and it made her wonder if a love that bloomed so quickly could live forever. "You smell good." She pushed her nose into the crook of his neck and inhaled. "You look good, too. I don't think I've ever seen you in a polo shirt before. I like your arms out. It's very sexy."

"You've seen me naked before. Me in a shirt is sexier?"

"Mmm-hmm." She just held on to him, enjoying this closeness. There had been no danger since she had been back here, but for the first time in a week she felt safe, protected.

"What did you tell your mother?" He smoothed his hand down her back.

"Nothing. I left her a note. My grandmother knows, though. She was eavesdropping on our conversation."

"We didn't say anything dirty, right?"

"No." She laughed. "What did you tell your mother?"

"The truth. But then again, she was eavesdropping on me, too."

"I think your mother and my grandmother would get along well."

"I'm sure they will. How long can you stay?"

"The whole night. I just need to be back by six. My grandmother may know what I'm up to, but I don't need my mother to know yet."

"She loves your ex, doesn't she?"

"Like a son. She took the breakup harder than I did."

"It's hard to get over your daughter's first love," he said and she laughed. She pulled away slightly to look up at him. She could see the exhaustion in his face. She knew he had worked late last night. He probably hadn't gotten any sleep.

"Let's go to bed." She took his hand. "Show me where we'll be sleeping tonight."

"You just want to sleep? You don't want me to make love to you?"

"I'll always want that and we can. I just thought you were tired. I know you didn't get much sleep yesterday."

He nodded. "I'm tired, but I want you." He took her face in his hands and looked into her eyes for a long moment before he kissed her gently. Her heart pulled painfully. He had been touching her that way since the day they met and it never failed to give her flutters and butterflies and every other girly emotion there was out there.

He broke the kiss slowly and she stood there with her eyes closed for a long moment. "You're so good at that. It just makes me want to say damn."

He gave a small chuckle and took her hand. "Let's go to bed."

"To sleep? Or to bed?"

"To sleep. I know you've had a long day, too." He led her to the large master suite that was beautiful in a sleek way but didn't have that homey feel. The décor of the house didn't match the block it was on.

"Don't deny yourself on my account." She looked at the enormous bed they were about to climb into. "I'm happy to do all the work while you lie back and enjoy."

"It's not just about sex with us."

"No." She tossed her purse on the dresser, pulled off her dress and kicked off her sandals. "But it's very good, though."

"We talk and we do things together and we like each other."

She wasn't sure where he was going with this. "I wouldn't be here if we didn't."

"Sometimes couples just sleep together."

"I know, which was my suggestion in the first place."

"I'm just letting you know that this is not a fling for me."

"Are you telling me or yourself that?"

"Both."

She blinked at him. "I'm not sure what you are getting at here."

"I'm not sure, either." He shook his head.

"Should we have a where-is-this-going conversation?" It had just been a month, but this felt serious. This felt like something that wouldn't burn out in a few weeks.

"Yes." He pulled his shirt off over his head. "But not tonight. Since I saw you this afternoon the only thing I've really wanted to do was crawl into bed with you."

She took a step closer to him and smoothed her hands over his bare chest. "I've missed the sight of this. I think you would do well down here. It's eighty degrees in the winter. You could go days without wearing a shirt."

"What if I gained fifty pounds and lost all my hair?"

"Then I would dump you like a bag of garbage." She

grinned at him just before she leaned in to kiss him. "It doesn't matter what you look like. It's the way you treat me that matters. It took a long time for me to realize that." She unhooked her bra, revealing her body to him. She noticed the way his eyes swept over her figure, taking it in as if he had never seen it before. Hallie had never felt so confident about her body before, but things had changed with Asa.

There was appreciation in his gaze and she was beginning to think she was becoming addicted to seeing him enjoy seeing her.

"Can you give me something to sleep in?"

He nodded and turned away from her and she climbed into the massive bed. It was supremely comfortable and even though she knew that her body was humming with arousal she could feel the sleepiness settling in. It had been a long, emotional day.

He handed her a T-shirt, crawled into bed beside her and as soon as she was done putting on his shirt he reached for her. "This bed." He groaned. "Is it just me or is this bed something special?"

"It is good." She shut her eyes and settled deeper into the mattress. "How was the rest of your day?"

"Good. Good… My sister is pregnant."

"Really?" She opened her eyes and looked up at him. He looked peaceful and she knew that in a few moments that he would be out cold. "Your family must be so excited."

"They don't know yet."

"What! How do you know and why are you telling me?"

"I got off the ferry today and took one look at her and just knew something was different. I can't explain how but I just knew. She isn't announcing it till their big Christmas party. I've got to keep the secret."

"You didn't, though. You just told me."

"Of course I told you. I tell you everything. Just don't tell anyone else."

"Damn. There goes the full-page ad I was going to take out in the paper."

He smiled, his eyes still closed. "I guess I knew that this day was coming, but it's still weird to know the person you used to share a crib with and who used to cry when you threw spiders at them is going to be someone's mother."

"Your sister is going to be a wonderful mother."

"I know. We're competitive. I think I might have to have a kid just to prove that I can out-parent her."

"Are you serious?"

"Only a little. I didn't think men had fantasies about their future families and kids, but I guess I did. Whenever I thought about having a family, I pictured my kids growing up with my sister's kids. Which is not something that's possible because her life is here and mine is in New York."

"I've always pictured raising my children here," she quietly said, knowing that he loved his life in New York while she merely tolerated it. "I'm not sure I could raise them anywhere else."

He made a soft noise and pressed his lips to her forehead. She wanted to know what he was thinking. Of course it was too early to be having a conversation about kids and where they saw themselves. Today was the first time she'd called him her boyfriend. But he had to know that New York wasn't permanent for her. Hideaway Island was. New York had been an adventure but this place was home.

"How was the rest of your day?" he asked her.

She inhaled deeply. "Up and down."

"Why? I thought you went shopping with your cousin."

"I did. I ran into my ex."

"Oh?" He opened his eyes.

"He said he wants to talk."

His face looked perfectly neutral, but she knew that his feelings didn't match. "What did you say?"

"Nothing. I walked away. I couldn't pretend like everything was okay between us after how badly it ended."

"Have you spoken to him since you broke up?"

"No. I moved to New York."

"Has he tried to contact you?"

"About three months ago. But I didn't answer. We're done. I wanted him to get that message. It's kind of hard when he and my mother are still so close. He visits the house a lot. I didn't realize how much until my grandmother told me. Luckily, he was away on business for the past week and didn't ambush me at the house."

"He knows you aren't going to be there the other times he visits. Maybe he just likes your mother."

"He loves my mother. He's not very close with his own. I think they are plotting to get us back together."

"Did you tell him you were seeing someone?"

"No."

"Did you tell your mother you were seeing someone?"

"You know I haven't yet."

"Maybe you would have avoided all of this if you had just told them." He was trying to keep his voice even but Hallie knew he was irritated with her.

"It doesn't matter if I have a boyfriend or not. The thing that should matter to them is what I want instead of conspiring against me and treating me like they both know what's best."

"How is your ex supposed to know what you want if you don't tell him? Tell him to back off. Tell him there's no hope. Talk to him."

"I don't want to talk to him. I'm still mad."

"You shouldn't be holding on to feelings from a relationship that is long over."

"That was five years of my life. I'd had the final fitting for my wedding dress. Our plane tickets for our honeymoon had been purchased. We'd put a down payment on a house. I'm not supposed to be angry about all of those plans we had being destroyed in one second without seeing it coming? If he wasn't happy he should have told me a long time before then. I think he owed me that."

"I don't think you're over him."

"I am over him, damn it! I'm just not done being angry yet."

"Why are you talking to me about this anyway? The last thing the new boyfriend wants to hear about is the ex."

"I'm telling this to you because you're not just the person I'm sleeping with, you're my friend and the person I turn to when I'm feeling sad or hurt or scared. I'm telling you this because I thought I could talk to you about everything."

"You can."

"But not about this." She shook her head. "That was a big part of my life before you, and—" "

He cut her off her with a kiss. She knew he only kissed her because he no longer wanted to talk about her past. He didn't want to start a fight. She wanted to keep talking about it. But why? What did that say about her? Did she still have feelings for her ex?

But Asa kept kissing her, his tongue sweeping into her mouth. His hands wandered her body and she forgot every other thought she had. There was no point thinking about the past when her present felt so damn good.

Chapter 15

Carlos arrived at Asa's rental home at seven thirty the next morning. Hallie had left two hours before. She refused to let him drive her home, for fear of waking up her mother. He had a funny feeling about him and Hallie. He couldn't describe it, but it was there—a knot in the pit of his stomach.

Uncertainty.

Her family hadn't known anything about him. They were still too tied to her ex. They wanted her back home for good. He had to believe her when she said she was no longer in love with her ex. He had to trust her. He really wanted to. But she wasn't over her breakup. She wasn't willing to trust him not to hurt her, either.

He might lose her to her ex, to the pull of this beautiful island.

It would kill him if he lost her, but how could he compete with so many years of history? With her family? With her home? It seemed like he was on the end of a losing battle.

"Thanks for agreeing to go on a run with me," Carlos said to him as they left the house and ran down the road toward the beach. "I need someone who's able to keep up with me. Virginia is up for a lot but she told me the only running she does is after a food truck."

"That sounds like her," Asa said, pulling his attention away from his troubling thoughts. "I haven't gone for a run in months." Asa really enjoyed his brother-in-law's company. He had been a little starstruck when Virginia first brought him home for Thanksgiving two years ago. But Carlos had no celebrity ego. He'd helped shovel the driveway. He'd cooked breakfast for them and was fine sleeping on the creaky twin bed in the guest room. Even if he hadn't been so down-to-earth, Asa probably would have liked him. Every other guy Virginia had brought home was a disaster.

"No? How have you been keeping in shape?"

"I work out with the firefighters, but my job keeps me in shape. It has been back-to-back large-scale disasters these past couple of months." They fell silent as they headed onto the empty beach. Hideaway Island was something else. He knew there were thousands of people on this little island, but even the more populated side of town felt deserted and peaceful. All he could hear was the sound of their feet hitting the sand and their even breathing. Each time he returned, he fell a little more in love with it.

He had heard Hallie when she'd said that she wanted to raise her children here. He understood why she felt that way. He was sure this was a wonderful place for that, but New York was, too. There was so much culture to expose his children to there, so many different types of people.

"Would you leave your job if you had another one lined up?"

"I haven't really thought about leaving, but it seems harder and harder for me to pull myself out of the house and go these past few months. I'm only trained in the medical field. I don't know what else I would do."

"How about work with athletes?"

"What do you mean?" He slowed down and looked at Carlos.

"I'm starting a foundation. I met this girl last year who is an amazing pitcher. Probably one of the best that I've ever seen, male or female. She could give some major-leaguer a run for their money. But she lives here on this island and there's not a lot of opportunity for her. There's no team here at her level. She has to play on travel teams off the island and the cost to her parents is a lot. Softball is her only shot at paying for college. I was lucky to grow up in a place where I had access to everything. I want to help out kids who don't."

"And what would you like me to do?"

"Run it. You were a scholar athlete. You know how hard it is to keep up your grades while playing competitively. My plan is to run an intensive camp here on the island in the summers where the kids could not only focus on sports, but academics and arts, too. Virginia will be teaching painting classes. You could run the day-to-day stuff and help me identify kids in need. I've been thinking about this for a long time and there is no one I trust more than you to help me run this."

"I'm honored. Man… I don't know what to say."

"I know it's a lot to take in right now. I'm asking you to give up your career and move away from a city you love, but I think you'll love this place, too, and I think you'll be great at it."

"Can I think about it?"

"Take all the time you need."

He was going to need time because for the first time in his life he had no idea what he was going to do.

* * *

Hallie sighed with pleasure as Asa kissed the inside of her thigh later that afternoon. She didn't ever think she would get tired of feeling this good.

They were both able to get away from their families for a few hours between activities and sneak away. They had gone to the private beach at the end of his road. It was completely empty, except for the two of them. They had played in the warm water and Hallie had dug her toes in the sand. She cherished the feeling of having her feet not confined in shoes and thick socks. The cool, wet sand was like an aphrodisiac, the familiar but no-longer-often-felt sensation sending tingles up her body. Or maybe it was the fact that Asa had been there with her, looking amazing in his blue bathing suit, with his arms and chest bare. The only time she saw him undress in New York was in bed, but here on Hideaway Island he looked delicious with the water beading on his skin and the sun shining down on him.

Her attraction to him wasn't fading; if anything it was growing stronger. She had reached for him, wrapping her whole self around him as she kissed him. Things had gone from hot to explosive and they barely made it back to the house. They certainly hadn't made it to the bedroom. They were on the rug in the living room. His lips getting closer and closer to her core. Little kisses and nibbles that were starting to make her squirm. She was ready for him. She always was. She didn't need much foreplay with him. But he was always so considerate. He had always taken his time; he always made sure she was shaking with need before he took her.

"Asa… Now. Please."

He lifted his head and shifted his body so that it hovered over hers. "Why do you always rush me?" he said with a little satisfied smile on his face. He bent and took her nipple in his mouth. "You know," he said while his mouth was still on her, "I like to take my time with you." The combination of his warm, wet mouth and his breath on her nipple drove her crazy.

"I've wanted you all day. Don't make me wait any longer."

He kissed her, taking her lower lip between his teeth. "Fine." He reached up with one arm to the coffee table, his hand reaching for his wallet. He took a condom out and flung his wallet across the room, which caused her to giggle.

"You think that's funny?" he asked, kissing her again. "You rush me and then have the nerve to giggle when I rush."

"I…" *I love you, Asa*, nearly slipped from her lips. It was true. She loved him. She was in love with him. But she stopped herself from saying it. She didn't think it was possible to fall out of love with one man and in with another in the span of a year, but she had gone and done it.

"You what?"

"I'm glad you're here. I'm so glad to be spending Christmas with you."

An hour later Hallie was slipping on her dress, preparing to go back to her parents' house. But she looked back at Asa who was lounging on the sofa, a throw blanket covering his nudity. He looked so gorgeous lying there, the rays of the afternoon sun hitting his face.

"I've got to go." She leaned down to kiss his lips.

"Don't." He grabbed her, pulling her down on top of him. She didn't resist, just went slack, enjoying the feel of his hard body against hers.

"I've got to." She pressed her nose into the seam of his neck. He smelled like ocean air and aftershave and a little bit like her. "I'm supposed to be making Christmas cookies with my family. We bring them to the senior citizen home."

"Fine. Leave me. Go do nice things for the elderly and leave me to languish here on my own."

"I thought you were here to see your family."

"I could see them—" he took his face in his hands and pressed his lips to her "—but I find you much cuter."

She closed her eyes and savored the feeling of his lips on hers, the closeness they shared. "Come home with me then."

"Seriously?" His eyes had widened and she knew her invitation was totally unexpected.

"You don't have to, if you don't want." She shook her head and tried to climb off him. She hadn't meant to ask him to come, but the words had slipped out of her mouth. "I just thought you could meet my mother and Nanny."

"Why are you getting all squirrely?" He wrapped his arms around her waist and kept her where she was. "Yes, I want to meet your family."

"You do?"

"Of course I do. Where else am I going to hear all those embarrassing childhood stories?"

She looked at him, studying his face carefully, and she believed him. Relief filled her. "Good. Get dressed quickly. We've got to head to the store. You can't show up without bringing Nanny a gift."

They stopped and got flowers and her grandmother's favorite sherry before they arrived at her parents' house. She had always loved walking up to her childhood home with its white picket fence and beautiful blooming bushes filled with flowers of every color. The house itself was done in pale salmon and soft sand-colored shades. There were ocean-blue accents here and there and intricate hand-carved latticework.

"It looks like a big gingerbread house," Asa said, sounding awed.

"That's exactly what my father was going for." And it was all decorated for Christmas. Last year they hadn't bothered with the decorations because no one felt much like celebrating, but this year her mother had pulled out all the stops and used all the things her father had made over the years. There was an enormous wreath on the door with golden starfish and seashells. To the side of the house there was a snowman that looked like it had melted into a puddle and all that was left was a head, his gloves, a mitten and a top hat. There were the wooden Christmas trees that her father and Derek had done together years ago. They were made of recycled beach fence wood and painted in various colors.

Looking at them now she recalled that this was how Derek had gotten his start in the furniture business. He'd begun selling these handmade trees to tourists as a teenager. It was how he'd put himself through college. Hal Roberts had been like a father to Derek, who had a strained relationship with his own father The bond between them was strong. She knew Derek took the loss just as hard as she did.

She felt Asa's hand on her shoulder. "Are you regretting bringing me here?"

"Of course not." She shook her head, feeling emotional. "No. I was just thinking about my dad."

"Holidays are hard." He kissed her forehead.

"This one is better." She should have realized that things with Brent were going to end last Christmas. She had just lost her father. The grief was nearly choking her and Brent wasn't there. Not emotionally or physically. He had missed her father's wake, was late for his funeral because he was away on business. Her family had been there, but she had felt alone. What she had needed was him to support her. What she got were excuses as to why he was too busy to be with her.

Asa kissed her forehead again, a reminder that he was there. Ever since he'd come into her life he seemed to be there exactly when she needed him.

The front door opened and her grandmother stood there with Derek. "I would ask who this is, but I'm pretty sure this is the man you sneaked out of the house to be with."

"Nanny!"

"Oh, don't be such a prude. Your mother is in the kitchen and she can't hear." Nanny's eyes took Asa in for a very long moment. Hallie glanced at Derek, seeing that he was trying hard not to laugh but was losing the battle. "Come here, young man." Nanny crooked her finger.

Hallie held her breath as Asa walked over to her. She didn't know why but she had been nervous ever since she'd made the suggestion to him.

Brent was a local. Their families had always known each other, but this was the first time Hallie had brought an outsider home.

"Hello, ma'am. My name is Asa. It's a pleasure to meet you." He handed her the bottle of sherry. "Thank you for having me in your home."

"Polite." She nodded her head in approval. "Tall, wide shoulders, well-built," she said as if she were ticking off a checklist. "Handsome as all get-out. Do you have a job?"

"Yes, ma'am. I work for the FDNY."

She nodded. "Heroic." She looked at Hallie. "How did you meet him again?"

"He came to my rescue when I hit my head on the ice."

"Aha. Is he a good kisser?"

"He's the best, Nanny. Gives me all kinds of butterflies and flutters."

"Nanny, can we be done with this inquisition?" Derek shook his head, looking uncomfortable. "I'm sure you're embarrassing the man."

"I can handle it. Go on, Hallie. Tell her some more good things about me," Asa said with a grin.

Hallie walked up the steps and stood next to Asa. She slipped her hand into his, locking her fingers with his. "Can I keep him, Nanny?"

"I say yes, but you need to ask your mother first. Go get her and put this bottle of sherry away, too."

"Yes, ma'am."

"Now you, Asa…" Nanny looped her arm with his. "You are going to have a nice little visit with me before we get started baking cookies. You do realize you are going to be baking cookies today? You will get your hands dirty. I hope you don't fuss about getting a little flour on your shirt or getting dough under your manicured fingernails."

"I came to work."

"Good. Hallie," she said without looking at her. "Why are you still standing there?"

"I'm going. I'm going." Nanny liked him. Hallie was relieved. Derek had liked him, too. She just had to get her mother on board.

Hallie ran into her halfway through the living room. "Oh, you're home. Is that sherry?"

"It's for Nanny. I brought a friend over to meet her." Hallie swallowed hard.

"You did?"

"And for you to meet, too."

"Oh?"

"It's a man. A man I've been seeing for some time now."

"You brought a man home for me to meet?" Clara stood there for a moment, clearly blown away by Hallie's statement. "That must mean it's quite serious."

"It is, or at least I think it's getting to be."

"Hallie?" Asa stepped inside. "Your grandmother would like the lavender lemonade. Hello, Mrs. Andersen. I'm Asa. It's very nice to meet you." He presented the orange lilies he had picked out for her.

"This is him?"

"Yes."

"This is who you went to have drinks with?"

"Yes."

"Well, he certainly is beautiful."

"I think so, too. Remember when you asked me if I had a man in my apartment that time?"

"I do."

"I did. This is him."

"You're the neighbor, aren't you? The paramedic she's always talking about."

"I am."

"And you've been dating my daughter and it's serious?"

"Yes to both."

Clara pushed the flowers at Hallie. "Put these in water for me, sweetheart, and bring the lemonade like your grandmother said." She was still looking at Asa as if she couldn't believe he was real.

Hallie looked back as Asa. She almost didn't want to leave him there alone.

"It's okay, baby. Go on," he said, reading her mind. "I'm fine."

She nodded once before she headed into the kitchen. There was a fresh pitcher of the lavender lemonade her grandmother was so fond of. Her mother always kept chopped vegetables and fruit in the fridge for snack. There was some cheese Hallie had bought still in there, so she decided to make a little tray for them to snack on.

The kitchen door opened and Brent walked inside just

like he always had when they'd been dating. But only they weren't dating now and he was the last person she wanted to see. Especially today when Asa was in the next room. Especially the day after Asa had accused her of still loving him. "What are you doing here, Brent?"

"Your mother invited me over to make cookies."

"We have plenty of help. You aren't needed." She went back to the tray she was putting together. She had hoped to hear the screen door shut behind him but it didn't and when she looked up again he was standing there staring at her. "You're not here to help. You've never once made cookies with us in the five years we were together. So say what you have to say so we can get this over with."

"I want you back and I'll do whatever it takes to get you back. My life has been miserable without you."

When they'd first broken up, she had longed to hear those words. Hear that he had made a mistake, that he had been stupid, but now that she was hearing them she didn't want to. She was almost numb to them.

"I'm sorry, but it's over." She shook her head. "I've moved away. I've moved on. There's no going back for us."

"None of that is permanent. Half the town is telling me that they saw you kissing some guy in Costa's yesterday, but I'm not paying any attention to them because I know you and I know you still love me as much as I love you."

"You don't believe that I was kissing a man in Costa's?"

"No." He laughed. "I know you. You're not that kind of girl."

Not that kind of girl.

He had just said the exact worst thing to her. "What kind of girl is that, Brent?"

"You wouldn't make out with some man in public. It would be embarrassing."

This had been the problem with their relationship. She

had tried so hard to fit in some impossible mold that he'd created. He was supposed to be a changed man. If they got back together, it would just be more of the same. "To whom would it be embarrassing? You?" She took in a deep, slow breath. "I was kissing a man yesterday and I spent the night with him. In fact I've spent every night I can with him."

"I heard it was Virginia Bradley's brother. You've been hooking up with him since you've been home? Some sort of fling to get back at me."

"You still think everything is about you. Asa is not a fling. We met in New York."

Chapter 16

Asa walked into the kitchen after Nanny sent him to see what was taking Hallie so long. He stood still for a moment after he walked through the door. Hallie was there, her arms crossed over her chest. Her jaw tight. There was fire in her eyes. He had never seen his sweet Hallie so upset.

Across from her was the ex. It wasn't who he expected her to have spent so many years of her life with. Asa didn't have to know anything about him to see that he had money. Big, expensive watch on his wrist. Hair slicked back. Clothes that were just a little too sleek for an afternoon of baking. But more than that Asa saw the look in the man's eyes. There was hurt there, mixed with anger, but there was mostly love.

"You met in New York? Or did you really meet here? Were you hooking up before we broke up?"

Hallie recoiled as if she had been slapped him in the face. "Get out."

Brent must have known he had gone a step too far. The anger cleared from his face, replaced by regret. "I'm sorry. I know you would never have been unfaithful."

Brent's eyes went to Asa in the doorway and the man's

entire body stiffened. Asa knew he should have backed away as soon as he saw him there, but he couldn't force himself to leave. He walked into the kitchen and stood by Hallie. He was torn between punching the guy and feeling sorry for him. He looked miserable. He probably was miserable. Asa had spent one week without Hallie and he missed her to the point of pain. And they had only been together for a month.

Five years seemed like a lifetime.

"Tell him how we met," Asa said softly.

"He doesn't need to know. He broke up with me when I was in the middle of planning our wedding, our lives together. He blindsided me and he's accusing me of cheating on him? He doesn't deserve a thing from me."

Brent took a step forward but stopped when he saw Hallie's hand go up. "I regret that. I didn't mean it, but what am I supposed to think?"

"Go!"

"I messed this up." He shook his head. "I just want to talk."

"It's over. For good. I moved on."

"With this guy? A paramedic? He can't provide you with the kind of life I can. He doesn't know you like I do. He can't love you like I can."

"You don't know anything about him." She shook her head. "This conversation isn't going anywhere. If you won't leave, I will." She walked out, leaving Asa and Brent alone.

"If you really love her, you have a shitty way of showing it," Asa said. "I don't know you, but it seems like you love yourself way more than you have ever loved her."

Brent sneered at him. "Why are you even speaking to me? You're irrelevant."

He shrugged. "Maybe I am to you, but I'm the one she's going home with tonight."

Brent took a step forward as if he was going to try something.

"I wouldn't disrespect these nice people by fighting in their home," Asa said trying to keep his temper in check. "But if you try something I will take you down, and I'll make sure you don't get back up."

"It's time for you to go, Brent," Derek said from behind him. "Asa might be too good to knock you out in here, but I'm not. You've hurt her once. You don't get to do it again."

"I'm leaving, but this is not the end of this. I need to hear her tell me that she's not in love with me anymore."

"I'm telling you," Derek said. "She's not."

"If she isn't, then why is she still so angry with me? There are feelings still there and I'm going to prove it to you all."

He stormed out then.

"Sniveling little brat." Derek practically spit out the words.

"Do you think he has a point?"

"What? Do I think she's still in love with him?" Derek paused for a moment, growing thoughtful. "I don't think she had been happy for a long time. But after her father died, she held on to the relationship because she didn't want to go through another big loss so soon. If his business had stayed small and he'd committed to having a simple life on this island, they would still be together. But he changed and everything became about money and work. He wasn't there when she needed him the most. She feels betrayed. It's hard to get over that."

Her father had died and the man she thought she was going to marry had broken up with her in the same year. Two hard blows back-to-back. Maybe she was right to ask for space. She said she had wanted time, and he had tried to give it to her, but destiny or fate or something had brought them together on this island for Christmas and he couldn't imagine going back to a life without her.

Hallie walked back into the living room to see her mother and grandmother standing there. The look of guilt on her mother's face was undeniable.

"I'm sorry, Hallie."

"Why did you invite him here?"

"I thought you guys might reconnect. I didn't know you were going to bring your boyfriend here."

"It doesn't matter if you knew or not. You knew he hurt me. You knew he was never there for me and yet you continued to see him, to welcome him here like nothing happened. Like I didn't have to go through the humiliation of canceling our wedding after all the invitations had gone out. I quit my job. I moved to New York. I've done everything to move on with my life and you've just invited him back in."

"He wants you back."

"Who cares? He wouldn't be here unless you made him think we had some kind of shot. If moving a thousand miles away didn't tell you something, I don't know what will."

"I just wanted you back here, sweetheart. I wanted you to spend the rest of your life in a place I know you love."

"Unfortunately my life is not about what you want." Hallie rubbed her head, her thoughts not coming clearly. She just knew that she felt suffocated, that she wanted to get out of here.

"Take a walk with me." Asa came out of nowhere and grabbed her hand.

She nodded and soon they were on the sidewalk walking down the street away from the more populated side of the island. Asa didn't say a thing to her as they went. He just held her hand, his quiet presence calming her. It was exactly what she needed at exactly the right time.

He was always exactly what she needed at the exactly the right time.

She hadn't realized where they were headed until she stopped in front of the little boathouse at the end of a deserted harbor. Of course she'd come here. This was a place only she and her father had ever gone. Their little secret, he'd called it.

"Where are we?" Asa finally asked as he looked at the nondescript house.

"My very special thinking place." She stepped forward and removed the key from the head of the wooden owl her father had carved when she was thirteen, and let them inside. The house was tiny, directly on the water, nothing protecting it from Mother Nature if she decided to unleash her fury. Hallie was surprised it was still standing after all these years, but it was. Her tiny little piece of paradise.

It was small on the inside, not meant for anyone to live there, merely built to store a boat below and entertain some guests before or after a day of sailing. But her father had built her a bed made from an old rowboat and a little couch that was suspended from the ceiling with two sturdy ropes. There were huge French doors that led out to the deck that overlooked the harbor and two huge, comfy armchairs that were perfect to curl up and read a book in.

"My father used to bring me here on rainy days," she said to Asa. "This was our special place. He used to sit at his desk." She pointed to a desk that folded in the wall when it wasn't in use. "I would read, or write in my journal while he worked. Sometimes I would just nap. The kitchen is small, but everything works. We would have chicken noodle soup. The kind from the can that is too salty, and peanut butter and jelly sandwiches."

"That sounds good," he said as he walked over and pulled her into a tight hug. "You want to have that for dinner tonight?"

It was just the right thing to say. Her eyes filled with tears and she shut them as she held on to him. "Yes, that sounds perfect."

"Then that's what we'll have."

"I've never brought anyone here before."

He was quiet for a long moment. "Does it feel weird?"

"No," she said truthfully. "I stayed here for a little while after the breakup. It felt so empty. I kept looking up, expecting to hear the scratching of his pencil on his sketch pad, but there was just silence. It doesn't feel empty right now."

"Tell me more about it."

"He left it to me. He wrote me a letter that his lawyer gave to me when the will was read. I can't get through it without falling to pieces."

"What does it say?"

"That he set aside provisions for my mother and grandmother to be taken care of for the rest of their lives, but that he left me everything else, because I was everything to him. He said he had never wanted children. His work had been enough, but when I was born I changed all that. He said I was his legacy. He told me that this place was mine to do what I wished with it. That I could bulldoze it or turn it into a burger joint, but he hoped that I kept it and that I only brought people here that were as special to me as I was to him."

Asa was that special to her, she realized. She had suspected that he was different than every other man she had known, but she hadn't been sure if it was love or lust, or some kind of crazy magnetism that had her wanting him so much. But standing there she knew, and suddenly nothing else mattered. Not the hurt Brent had left her with. Not her mother taking his side. All that mattered was the new love that she shared with this man.

"I wish I could have known him, Hallie. I think I would have liked him a lot."

She knew her father would have liked Asa, too. Maybe it was divine intervention. Maybe her father had sent this man to love her. She had been in this boathouse when she decided to move to New York. Here she had first come across the ad for her apartment on that website. She had moved to the Village, where her father had gotten his start, only to move into Asa's building, and when that wasn't enough she had fallen, and Asa had gotten the call to come pick her up. And now he was here on Hideaway Island, not letting her forget about him, making her fall in love with him more and more each day. Fate and destiny were too hard to fight.

"You're being so good to me."

"I'm not being good to you. I'm being the man I'm supposed to be."

"You are. You're being better than I would be. You're not going to ask me about Brent? You're not going to make me swear to never see him again? You're not going to act all macho and jealous?"

"No."

"What if I want you to do all that?"

"If you want to speak to Brent, I wouldn't try to stop you. I don't own you. You have to decide what's best for you."

What was best for her?

Staying here with her family on the island that she so dearly loved or going back to New York to be with a man who took care of her in every way that she had ever dreamed.

The indecision was making her dizzy. So she shut off her mind and decided to live in this moment for as long as she could.

She looked up at Asa, deep into his eyes. "Will you take a nap in my boat bed with me?"

He smiled down at her softly. "How did you know that that was exactly what I was hoping you would ask?"

"Are you ready to give up your spacious house for a small cottage?" Asa asked his father a few days later as they walked through the third house they had seen that day. His mother was in deep discussion with the Realtor and Asa and his father were left alone to go through the house once again.

"I'm old. I hate shoveling snow and mowing the lawn. So yes, son. I am ready to live in a little beach cottage."

"I'm having a hard time wrapping my head around this. I liked the idea of knowing that you and Mom were just a couple of hours away in New Jersey. Now I'm going to have to fly to see you."

"We talked about this, you know." His father walked ahead of him to look in the master bedroom closet. "Your mother and I." His father had been retired from the military for many years and yet he had never lost his colonel-like bearing. But here on Hideaway Island, he turned into a much more relaxed man. "We debated leaving you behind in New York alone. And then we remembered that you're a grown man and that you could take care of yourself better than anyone. Plus we know how much you love your job."

"Yeah," he said. Only when he thought about his job lately, love wasn't the feeling that came to mind. He had been off for five days now. There was no blood, no gunshots, no horrific accidents, no crying victims. It was nice to go days without seeing someone in extreme pain, without seeing someone at their worst.

Carlos had offered him that job, but Asa was having a hard time entertaining the idea of him running a foundation. He'd become a rescue paramedic because he loved the action, the adrenaline he felt when the sirens went on and they were rushing toward a scene. He hated being bored. And he didn't want to risk taking such a big job only to leave it when his dissatisfaction began to creep up.

"What's the matter, son? You thinking about that girlfriend of yours?"

He wasn't, but he smiled at the mention of her. "She was grilling me this morning about what to get you for Christmas."

"I haven't even met the girl yet and she's buying me a Christmas present."

He nodded. "She had already gotten Mom and Virginia theirs. She didn't want you to feel left out."

"Your sister says she's sweet."

"She is. I love her."

Colonel Andersen nodded. "Your sister also told me that. I've never heard you say that about a woman before."

The words slipped out of Asa's mouth easily. He had told his sister and parents of his love but he had yet to say it to Hallie. He could have. There were a thousand times he could have told her, especially since she had stopped staying at her childhood home and had moved in with him. He felt a little guilty that he liked the fact that her days started and ended with him since she had gotten into that argument with her mother. She still saw them. They went over together and ate with them. There was an afternoon of card playing with all of Hallie's aunts. They just did it as a couple. She left with him every evening, never allowing herself to be alone with her mother.

He felt bad that she was upset with her mother during the holidays when she had looked so forward to coming home, but it was tough being here, too. She was still grieving for her father. He didn't realize how much until she took him to the boathouse. There was raw, naked pain in her eyes that day and it made him feel hollow. It made him realize how lucky he was to have two healthy, vibrant parents. He was going to miss them when they moved. He was starting to regret that his job prevented him from spending more time with them.

"Now that you're back from your little spontaneous road trip with your friends, you can meet Hallie tonight."

"I was sure I was going to meet her today on our house search. She knows this island well and her father designed some of the homes here."

"She didn't want to intrude. She took her grandmother out for lunch."

"Do you have anything special planned for her for Christmas? Maybe a special piece of jewelry and an important question to ask?"

Marriage.

It would be a lie to say that he hadn't thought about it a hundred times in the last few days.

He could see her as the mother of his children. He could imagine waking up every day with her next to him. Especially since that afternoon they'd spent in the boathouse. They had lain huddled together in that little boat bed and just talked about everything, about nothing, for hours. He had never felt so close to another person in his life. But… "I'm not sure if it's the right time."

"It's soon. I know. But if you love her and she makes you happy, why wait?"

It was a good question. But he just wasn't sure Hallie was ready. She needed to close the last chapter of her life before they entered into a new one.

Chapter 17

Asa watched Hallie as she fussed with her dress, twisting this way and that as she studied herself in the mirror. It was Christmas Eve, the night of the party at Virginia and Carlos's house. Hallie wore red, of course. A deep red one-shoulder gown that skimmed her body in just the right places. She looked like a goddess with a halo of curls. His damn heart beat faster. He wasn't sure he would be able to make it the entire night without touching her.

"You're gorgeous. Stop worrying." He got up and walked toward her. "You'll make people's jaws drop when you walk in tonight."

"You have to say that. You're my boyfriend." She turned to face him, tilting her head to one side as she looked up at him. "We both might have a case of love goggles. Do you ever think about that? I could be so attracted to your spirit that you could have bad teeth, pimple-filled skin and a beer belly and I wouldn't even be able to tell because your inner beauty has me blinded."

"No." He couldn't suppress his smile. She could be silly sometimes. He loved that about her. No one else had ever made him smile so much. "I never think about that." He slipped his hand into the pocket of his suit and pulled out a small black box. "Your ears look cold." He pulled out the diamond hoop earrings that were unique and classic at the same time. "You said that you were going to have to borrow a pair of earrings from your mother before you went, but now you don't have to."

"They are beautiful." She touched her ears.

"You haven't even looked at them yet."

"I don't have to. I already know, because you picked them. I hardly have any good jewelry anymore."

"Why not?"

"I gave it all back," she said softly. To Brent. She didn't have to say any more. His presence hung between them. They hadn't spoken about him since they had that disagreement he ended by making love to her and Hallie seemed to be happy to go on the rest of her life never mentioning him again. But they weren't finished. There was no closure there.

No sure sign from Hallie that there were no lingering feelings.

She'd come to New York to escape her problems, to escape Brent, but he would always be here. Every time she came back he would be there, their issues never resolved, him continuing to think that she still loved him.

As much as he loved her, Asa didn't want to be her rebound. She had been dropping hints, speaking of their future as if they were definitely going to have one. *When we get back to New York… Let's go there this summer…* If she was coming back to New York, it would be for him. Not for any other reason and that should've made him feel good. But he didn't want to be the person she tried to forget her former love with. And he didn't want her making sacrifices for him. If she had loved New York and found another reason to stay, that would be one thing. He didn't want her to stay just for him, because in the end she wouldn't be happy. And it would be the same thing that had happened with Brent.

"Don't give these back." He reached in his pocket and pulled out her next gift. "This is your real present." It was a gold charm bracelet. "This is all the stuff we did this holiday season."

"There's a little ambulance." Her eyes filled with tears.

"For how we first really met. And a Christmas tree for that day we walked in the park. A train for the ride we took together. A gingerbread house for the ones we decorated in the castle. This last one is a lily to represent the ones that grow wild all over this island, where we ended up for the holiday."

She really started to cry then, not just tears streaming down her face, but full chest-heaving crying.

"Honey, why are you crying?" He smoothed his hand down her back as he held her.

"You know why."

"You like your present?"

"It makes mine look like crap."

He laughed. "I'll love it. I know I'll love it."

"This hurts, you know. The amount of what I feel for you is so much that it hurts."

"I know," he whispered. "I've never felt this way about anyone before. I almost don't know how to handle it."

"You don't have to handle it." She looked up at him. "Just be with me."

He nodded and wiped away the tears that were rolling down her cheeks. "We've got to get going."

"My face is a mess, isn't it?"

"No. I think it's just perfect."

A half hour later they had arrived at his sister's oceanfront mansion. Virginia and Carlos didn't normally throw around their wealth, but tonight they weren't afraid to show off what they had because they had opened their homes to the entire island. This was a night that the people of Hideaway Island wouldn't forget.

The house looked like a Christmas wonderland. They had brought in white Christmas trees that had been decorated with ornaments in various shades of blue and silver winding up the long driveway. There were candles—hundreds and hundreds of flickering candles—lighting the paths that led to the back of the house where there were tents set up overlooking the beach. The first thing they were greeted with was a replica of the town made completely from gingerbread. It was all there—the historic church, the town square, even the post office—and the little edible buildings were all decorated for the holiday exactly like the real town had been.

"I'm amazed by this," Hallie said as she looked up at Asa. "Truly amazed by it all."

"My sister is amazing. She had a really small, intimate wedding in Costa Rica. So this is her making up for it."

"I'll say." Hallie's eyes traveled to the tables and tables of food around the room. Whole turkeys and hams. Trays of freshly caught fish and pasta and a dozen things she couldn't identify. One table just held candy, another a giant chocolate fountain.

Christmas music filled the air, provided by a band dressed in black tie and in the center of it all, in front of a large evergreen, stood Carlos and Virginia, looking dazzling and staring at each other like they were in love, like there was no one else in the world but them.

"Hallie." Asa touched her shoulder. "Your grandmother is trying to get your attention."

"Oh." She looked over to the bar where her grandmother was holding two glasses of champagne and staring at her. "I didn't even see her there."

"Go speak to her. I'm going to say hello to a few people."

* * *

Asa went over to his sister and brother-in-law, whom they had seen briefly when they first walked in. Virginia was in a white, flowy gown that managed to look beachy and perfect for winter at the same time. There was a white flower tucked into her curls and a smile on her face. He had never seen her look happier.

"Hey, twin." She hugged him. "I'm sorry I didn't get to do that earlier."

"Don't be. This place looks fantastic. All the planning was worth it."

"You think so? I just want everyone to have a good time. I want to thank them for everything they have done for us on this island to make us feel welcome."

"You succeeded."

"Good. How's Hallie? She looks like she was crying."

"She was, but please don't tell her that. We almost didn't make it because she thought she looked a mess."

"Why was she crying?" Virginia raised a suspicious eyebrow.

"She liked the present I gave her." But he knew it was more than that. She loved him. Or she wanted to love him and felt guilty about not being able to.

She cared deeply for him. That was the only thing he was sure of at the moment. There was so much uncertainty around them. He didn't want to push her to make a decision. He just wanted to be there. A quiet force showing her that he loved her, that his love was unwavering. That he would always be there for her when it mattered. He needed her to choose with her heart instead of her head. He wanted to force her to choose him, to rage at her for not knowing, to beat the hell out of Brent for existing, but he knew that wasn't the way to win her.

Being patient was by far the hardest thing he ever had to do.

"It was incredibly thoughtful. I didn't think you had it in you."

"It seems like things are getting pretty serious between you two," Carlos said.

"It seems like it."

"I think she's good for you, Asa." Virginia glanced over to where Hallie was. "Mom loves her. Daddy already is referring to her as his future daughter-in-law."

"What do you think about her?"

Virginia exchanged a look with Carlos and for a moment Asa's stomach dropped.

"I think that if you don't ask her to marry you, the entire family will turn against you and I will forever be the favorite."

"So you like her?"

"No. I adore her. Don't waste any more time. You found her. Be happy with her."

That was the only thing he wanted, but he caught Brent in the corner of his eye and knew that once he spotted Hallie, he wasn't going to leave tonight without speaking to her again, trying once again to convince her to come back to him.

"What's the matter, Asa?" Carlos asked. "You look like you're gearing up for a fight."

"I'm not. But there is someone here I would love to knock on their ass."

"Who?" Carlos swiveled around, his shoulders growing broader. "We can go get him."

"No, you won't be going anywhere, dear husband." Virginia grabbed his hand. "Not until we announce our big news. Asa can handle himself." She looked up at him. "Who's got you wanting to do bodily harm?"

He motioned over to Brent, who even Asa had to admit was looking dapper tonight in a navy blue tux. "Hallie's ex."

Carlos's eyes hardened. "His agency sold me this house. His father, to be exact. If I had known, we wouldn't have invited him."

"Did it end badly?" Virginia asked.

"He told her he wasn't sure he loved her enough to marry her a few weeks before their wedding and now he wants her back. He's going to try to convince her to leave me tonight."

"I hope she tells him to go to hell."

"I hope she does, too."

Carlos shook his head. "You're going to let some other man try to take your woman?"

"He can try all he wants. I have to trust that Hallie will do what she needs to do if she wants to be with me." He said the words with conviction, but that didn't stop the little niggle of doubt inside him.

Chapter 18

"You look beautiful, Nanny." Hallie studied her grandmother as she approached her. Nanny wore a silver gown, her hair swept up in a simple but elegant way that made her look regal and classic. She didn't look anywhere near her eighty-two years and Hallie hoped that she looked a quarter as good as her grandmother did when she got to be her age.

"Thank you, my dear." She handed her a glass of champagne and touched her cheek. "You've been crying."

"Can you tell?"

"What happened?"

"Nothing. They were happy tears. Asa surprised me with a wonderful gift."

"An engagement ring?" Nanny's eyes lit with joy.

"No," Hallie said, surprised that she found herself disappointed. She had seen the black velvet box and for a moment she'd thought… But they were earrings, beautiful earrings. "He gave me these." She motioned to them. "And this. It's a charm bracelet. A charm for all the things that we have done together since we have met."

"How thoughtful."

"It was. Incredibly so."

"What would you have said if he had asked to marry you? I know it's soon and that you weren't prepared to be in a serious relationship again..."

"I would have said yes." There was no doubt in her mind. If he had asked, she would have said yes without a second thought.

"Said yes to what?" Her mother approached them then. She was wearing an emerald green gown that hugged her body in all the right places. Hallie had forgotten that her mother was a stunner. She could still turn heads and had a lot of years left ahead of her. Hallie didn't want her mother to spend the rest of her life alone.

"To Asa," she answered, distracted. "You look incredible, Mom."

"Really?" She nervously patted her hair. "It's not too much?"

"Too much what?"

"You know." Clara ran her hands down her hips. "Too much everything."

"You're a knockout," said Nanny. "I think you should start dating again."

"What?" She looked startled. "That came out of nowhere. And anyway, I couldn't."

"Yes, you can, daughter. It has been over a year. You married a man much older than you and while he gave you great happiness, he shouldn't be your only happiness. Hallie can't be the only thing good in your life. You need more. You need to let the girl do what she wants without your interference."

"But, Mother...." Clara seemed completely knocked off guard.

"I love you, Clara." Nanny pecked her cheek. "I'm going to find a gentleman to dance with. I'll see you two later."

She walked away, leaving Clara and Hallie alone for the first time since they'd had their argument.

"I guess we should talk," Clara said to Hallie in a soft voice.

"I guess we should. Let's go out to the beach where it's a little quieter."

It was a warm, breezy night and they both slipped off their heels and pulled up their gowns as they walked onto the cool sand. They were quiet for a while, listening as the waves gently crashed against the shore.

"I guess I should start by saying I'm sorry," Clara spoke first.

"You don't have to."

"I do because I am. I didn't think. I just wanted you to be happy. I didn't know you were seeing someone else."

"I wasn't happy with him and if I wasn't seeing someone else, that didn't mean I wanted to get back with Brent."

"I lost you and your father so close together. I was being selfish. I thought if you got back together you would stay here and start a family. I just don't know what to do with myself since your father passed away."

"Date. Go out dancing. Take a trip to the beach with a hunky man."

"Is that what you've been doing with Asa this week?"

"We've been having a very nice time here," she said sighing. "It makes me not want to leave the island again."

"But you will because of him."

"Yes. He puts me first. He's my rock and every time I look at him I get a little breathless. Life is just kind of gray without him."

Clara made a soft noise. "I feel that way about your father. My life is just gray now."

"I don't want that for you, Mom."

"I don't want that for me, either. I'm glad you found

Asa. He's a good man. Will you really be happy in New York? I know how much you love it here."

"I do," she said looking out at the moonlit ocean. "There's no place like it."

"Hallie, I want to say something to you and I don't want you to get upset. I just want you to listen."

Hallie was apprehensive, but she nodded, waiting for her mother to speak her mind.

"I know a big bone of contention between you and Brent was that he wanted to move to Miami and you wanted to stay here. You felt like you had given everything up for him already. Aren't you doing the same thing with Asa?"

"I'm not moving to New York for Asa. I was already there."

"But you are staying in a place that eight weeks ago you were sure you were going to leave. I know Asa is dear to you, but are you sure you want to compromise so much for a man you have known for such a short time?"

Her mother was right. Logically it all made sense even though she didn't want it to. She was so sure of her feelings for Asa, but that tiny bit of doubt in the back of her mind never really went away "If it doesn't work out I can always come home again. This place isn't going anywhere."

"No, of course not. But I don't want you running home to nurse another broken heart. I want you home because you want to spend your life here."

"The last thing I want is another broken heart. But I…"

"No," a man's voice said from behind her. "I guess I've already taken care of that."

She turned to see Brent standing there. Even she had to admit he looked beautiful that evening—sleek, expensive, probably a thousand women's dreams. But he wasn't her dream anymore and when she looked at him she didn't feel hurt, or angry, or sad. She felt nothing. That was the nicest feeling. There was nothing left there.

Realizing how much she loved Asa made all the other stuff that was lingering in the background disappear. "I should be getting back to Asa now. He's probably wondering where I am." She turned to leave but Brent grabbed her wrist.

"I just want to talk to you. Give me a chance. Give me five minutes."

Hallie looked at her mother, just to have somewhere else to look other than at Brent. "Mom, can you give us a minute?"

"Yes, I'll be inside. At the candy buffet, gnawing on a chocolate Santa." Clara squeezed Hallie's arm before she went.

Brent stood there awkwardly for a while, just staring at her. "You look very beautiful tonight, Hallie. I even like your hair short. It makes your eyes stand out."

She nodded. "Thanks."

"Let's walk. We've walked on this beach once before, remember? When my father first secured this listing."

"Let's walk back toward the house. You asked for five minutes. That's all I have left to give you."

"You used to be so agreeable before. You're a little more strong-willed now. I like that."

She started walking away, forcing him to keep up with her, not wanting to hear any more of his platitudes. "What do you want to talk about?"

"I want another shot with you. I know I've hurt you, but I got scared. I just needed time to think things over before we walked down the aisle, but eight months without you nearly killed me. I could barely function."

"You looked like you managed to get along fine."

"But I didn't. I feel terrible for what I did and if you

give me the chance, I will spend the rest of my life making it up to you."

"There's nothing to make up to me. I'm fine. Really, I'm happy now."

"The paramedic really makes you happy? I know I might not be as big or strong as him, but I can make you happy. I can give you the world. If you stay with him you'll be living in a shoebox-sized apartment and struggling to make ends meet on a city-worker's salary."

"This is not about Asa. I don't need the world. I need someone to love me, to be there for me."

"I can do that for you!"

"It's too late now. I could have taken you cheating. I could have put up with your endless quest for more money, but I just needed you there for me when my father died. That's when it counted, that's when it was important and you couldn't do that."

"I'm sorry about that. I didn't know how to be there for you. You were in so much pain. I was just going through some stuff. I broke up with you because I wasn't sure I could be there for you like that. I wasn't sure I could be the man I thought I should be with you, but I was wrong. The time did me good. I'm sure we'll be much stronger this time around."

"We had five years together and before that we dated in high school. You had plenty of time. You should have been sure of me, of us. But you weren't and that's okay, because neither one of us was happy. You did me a favor by ending it, because we would have gotten married and have been miserable and it wouldn't have been fair to either of us to go into a loveless marriage."

"Loveless? I loved you!"

"You said loved, not love. You loved me once, but somewhere along the way you fell out of love with me. And—"

"I didn't. I still love you."

"You love the idea of having a sweet, dependable wife. You love that I took care of you, that I was always there. But let's face it—that last year we barely touched. We didn't talk. There was convenience and companionship, but there was no passion and there certainly was no love, at least not the love that two people who are going to get married should have. You did me a favor by breaking up with me. I know what kind of relationship I want now. I'm not mad anymore. I'm not hurt. I just want to move on with my life and I want you to move on, too."

Brent was quiet for a long time as they made their way closer to the house. "I've spent the last few months planning how to get you back and in five minutes you destroy all those plans and all my hopes for the future."

"You're single, you're good-looking and you're rich. You'll find someone who is crazy about you. I'm sure there's already someone waiting in the wings. Or maybe a dozen women waiting in the wings. All you've got to do is crook your finger."

Brent shook his head and gave her a sad smile. "I wish it was that easy. It's going to take me a while to get over you. It wasn't all bad, was it?"

"No. I really did love you. It was real for me."

"But just not anymore?"

"No." She shook her head. "Not anymore. I'm sorry, Brent."

"Don't be sorry. Maybe we were supposed to go through this."

"Maybe."

He grabbed her and pulled her into a tight hug. "Thank you for those five years. You've made me a better man."

"You're welcome."

"You had better go. Your man is waiting for you."

"I should get back to the party."

"You don't have to go that far to see him. He's standing behind us."

Asa had gone looking for Hallie. The whole island was at the party, his family was there, but he was missing her beside him. He sought out Nanny, asking her where she might be, only to be informed that she had gone walking on the beach with her mother. He had been glad to hear that. He wanted Hallie to sort things out with her. He didn't want her to leave here with any unfinished business between them.

But a few minutes later he spotted Clara standing at the dessert bar alone. No sign of Hallie anywhere around her. "Hello, Mrs. Roberts." He approached her, still feeling a little awkward around her. He knew he wasn't her choice for her daughter, that he might never live up to what she had with Brent.

"Oh, hello, Asa. You look very dashing this evening."

"And you look very beautiful. I can see where Hallie gets it from."

"Thank you. You don't have to charm me, Asa. I already like you."

"Do you? And I wasn't trying to charm you. I was telling you the truth. Hallie has your eyes."

"And my husband's smile. And his ears, and his thoughtful nature." She sighed. "Will you dance with me, Asa?"

"Sure." He was a tiny bit hesitant but he took her hand and led her out to the dance floor where a slow jazzy Christmas carol was being played by the band.

"My daughter seems quite taken with you."

"I'm blown away by her."

"I see the way you look at her. Are you in love with my daughter?"

"Yes," he said without hesitation.

"And you're sure? After a month? Can you even say you know her well?"

"I am sure about her."

"Marriage, children. Do you know what she wants? Do you know what her dreams are for her life? How she's always envisioned her future?"

"I do. I know she's never wanted to live in New York. I know that she only came because she was trying to ease her broken heart. I know that she really wants to be here."

Clara was surprised. She stopped dancing and just looked at him. "You do know her."

"Of course I do." He took her hand again, and they started to dance again. "But I don't think she really knows what she wants. She'll come back to New York. She'll try to make a life with me because that's what she thinks I want. She thinks it will make me happy and I'm not sure I can allow her to do that. She has to know what she wants before we really move forward and make a life together."

Clara pulled away from him completely then. "You really are just what she needs. She should be coming up from the beach now. You should go to her."

He nodded and left the party, walking down the path that led to the private beach that surrounded Carlos and Virginia's home. A couple embracing on the path leading up to the house caused him to stop. It took him a few seconds to process what he was seeing. But it was Hallie, her arms wrapped around Brent. His arms were around her, too, and his eyes were closed. The look of love was clear on his face even though Asa couldn't see the man's eyes. It felt like a quick, brutal gut punch. He couldn't see Hallie's face. He didn't know what she would look like if he could see her, wasn't sure if that same look of love would be etched on her face.

He didn't want to be her stand-in, her replacement for Brent. He couldn't live with being her second choice, no matter how much he loved her.

They must have sensed that someone was watching them because they broke apart, exchanging a few quiet words before Hallie turned around to see him.

"Hi, baby." She smiled softly up at him and left Brent where he stood. "I was missing you."

She didn't have a guilty look on her face. She didn't seem likc she had been caught doing anything wrong. She looked at peace, almost happy. But why? Because she had just gained the closure that she needed? Or because she got to have a few private moments with the man she had loved for years.

"Hey, I was missing you, too."

"Good." She kissed his cheek. "There's a big plate of food with our names on it."

Chapter 19

There was just family left at the Bradleys' house around 1:00 a.m. The party had been a massive success, topped off when Virginia and Carlos had made the announcement that they were going to be parents. They had hired a Santa Claus to hand out gifts to the partygoers and each member of the family got the same exact present. A small framed picture of their first ultrasound. Dr. Andersen burst into tears. Carlos's mother screamed. Everyone was delighted by the news, the whole room filled with genuine joy. It was a very good Christmas, one of the best Hallie had ever had. The only thing that could have made it better was the presence of her father. But even though he wasn't with them physically, she felt him there in spirit.

"This was the perfect party," she said to Asa as she sat in his lap, her arms looped around his neck. They were in a corner, and various members of the Bradley/Andersen family were hanging out in the tent that overlooked the ocean. Only the lights from the Christmas tree and the glow of the moon illuminated the night.

"I agree. I'm so glad it didn't start raining until after the announcement." He looked out toward the ocean and she sensed something was off with him. He had been so incredibly quiet for the past couple of hours. "It's really coming down now."

"It's so peaceful here," she said following his gaze. "I love the sound of the rain on the island."

"Not at all like New York."

"No." She kissed his cheek and then down to his throat. "Although I will always have very fond memories of that peaceful night we spent upstate. I could easily live there, too, as long as you are there with me."

"Really? I'm not sure I would be happy with you moving someplace just for me."

"Why not?" She blinked at him, not sure she understood what he was saying.

"Because in the end, I don't think you would be happy."

"*You* make me happy," she told him.

"But I don't want to be the only thing to make you happy."

"What does that mean? I thought this is what you wanted. Isn't it? A commitment. A promise that I will be there for you like you have been there for me."

"Yes."

"Then what the hell are you trying to tell me?"

"Let's not talk about it tonight. Let's not ruin this evening."

"Do you want to ask me what happened with Brent on the beach? Is that what this is about?"

"You're damn right I want to ask you what happened with Brent. I want to know what he said to you and why he was hugging you. I want to know if you're still going to think about him after we leave here. I want to know where your heart is."

"You know where it is? I just told you that I would give

up my hometown and my family to be with you. What else can I say?"

"I—"

"Hallie." Derek was standing behind them, the tux he was wearing soaked by the rain. Fear was evident on his face and Hallie stood up and went to him, not wanting to hear what he was going to say but needing to know.

"It's your mother and Nanny. They were in a car accident on their way home."

The drive to the hospital was one of the longest of Asa's life and he knew that it wasn't his family in the car, but he still worried as if it were his mother and his grandmother whose car was totaled due to a slick spot on the road. He was so used to being on the other side, doing the drive to the hospital with an injured victim in the back. He had responded to dozens and dozens of car accidents; many times he didn't even make it to the ER before they lost the person they were working on. And suddenly they all came back to him, all those faces twisted in pain and fear. He had been addicted to the lights and sirens for a while, the rush of heading to the scene. But there was no rush this time, only fear. And seeing the woman he was in love with frozen in terror really made him reevaluate things. For the families of the victims he worked on, there was no shaking it off, no going back to business as usual.

The hospital on Hideaway Island was small, sleepy even. Most people went to Miami for their major medical care. And the fact that Nanny and Clara didn't have to be airlifted out was a good thing. Or it could mean the worst…

But he refused to let his mind go there. He took Hallie's hand and led her inside. He didn't try to reassure or say any comforting words, because he knew she wouldn't hear them. She had lost her father, and left her hometown. Her life had changed so much in the last year and now she was faced with the potential loss of even more. There were no words that were sufficient enough, so he just held her hand, squeezing her fingers to let her know that she wasn't alone.

Derek walked into the ER, right past the lone security guard and the front desk. He was the mayor of the town and no one dared to stop him as he looked for his grandmother and aunt.

"Excuse me, Mayor Patrick." A young nurse came up to them. "Your grandmother is in here."

They rushed into a small room to see Nanny sitting up in a hospital bed, her hand pressed to her head, holding a bandage in place. She looked okay, but Asa could see by the blood seeping through the bandage that she had injured her head.

"Oh, good, my family is here. Tell this child that I'm not going to let him go anywhere near my head with a needle."

"What's the issue?" Asa asked, glancing at Nanny's chart.

A young doctor looked up at him. Nanny wasn't exaggerating. He didn't look more than nineteen or twenty. Asa knew he had to be older, but he probably wasn't very experienced. "Mrs. Duvall needs several stitches. The wound goes from the top of her eyebrow up to her forehead and she's refusing to let me do it."

"That's because he's twelve!"

"Nanny," Hallie scolded. "Let him do his job. Where's Mom?"

A worried look crossed Nanny's face. "They are running tests. She took the brunt of the impact. Her arm was really hurting her."

Asa rubbed Hallie's back, still unable to find the right words to say to her. She leaned into him, the fear still clear on her face.

"Tell me what I can do for you," he whispered into her ear.

"Can you take care of Nanny while Derek and I try to find out what is happening with my mother?"

"Of course." He left Hallie's side and approached the older woman whose face was set with a mixture of pain and stubbornness. "Would you like me to do your sutures, Nanny?"

"You can do them?"

He nodded. "For a very short week I debated whether or not I should make plastic surgery my specialty before I left the program."

"And why didn't you?"

"I like my women with all natural parts. I couldn't see my entire career putting plastic parts in them."

"Noble." Nanny smiled, but he could tell the action hurt her head.

"I've done sutures hundreds of times. I've patched up firefighters and doctors and beautiful women such as yourself. I promise to do a good job. Or I can sit here and hold your hand while you let the good doctor do it?"

"You can do it." She sighed softly.

"Um, I'm not supposed to let anyone do my sutures for me," the young doctor said.

Asa looked around. The hospital was small and practically empty that Christmas Eve. "It will make her happy and who's going to know?"

"Thank you, baby." Hallie kissed his cheek and then left the room with Derek.

Christmas Day hadn't been what Hallie had been hoping or expecting. It was spent in the hospital with her mother and grandmother. Both women were going to be okay. Besides the nasty gash on her head, Nanny had a few bumps and bruises. Clara was worse off. Her arm was badly broken and needed surgery. She had two fractured ribs and she was in serious pain every time she took in a deep breath. She would need physical therapy and someone to look after her, which Hallie was happy to do, but she was glad to know that she wasn't alone in doing so.

Asa had been there with her the entire following week. Cooking and cleaning, fetching Nanny anything she wanted, keeping Clara occupied so she wouldn't get bored and try to get up and move. She was grateful to him, beyond grateful actually. She wasn't sure she would have been able to get through this week without him. Or his family. Carlos and Virginia came over to visit every day, and Asa's parents had stayed with Nanny and Clara so she and Asa could get out for a few hours. It wasn't the holiday she'd expected, but it wasn't a terrible one, because for the first time in a long time she hadn't felt like she was in it alone. She felt like part of a big, loving family.

But even with all the love and support she received from him, she couldn't help but think back to right before Derek had come to tell her the news about the accident.

He wasn't sure if she was in this for the right reasons. He wasn't sure if she was really going to be there for him like he had been there for her.

She had been angry with him in that moment and she would still be angry with him if this past week, he hadn't been his normal wonderful self.

He had been her rock, there when she needed him. It was like some sort of big, blaring message to her. *Don't lose him. Your heart won't be able to take it.*

But he was packing his bags, preparing to return to the life he had left behind in New York. This wasn't the end, he had told her. He just needed to get back to work.

But her stomach ached with dread, because she had a

feeling that this was the end. That he was never going to trust her to love him completely.

Maybe he was right to. Maybe she had dragged him into too much drama with her ex. Maybe he was better off back in New York, loving somebody else.

"I like the nurse we hired," he told her as he retrieved his boots from the closet at his rental home. His flight was tonight. He had to report for work at midnight the next day It was New Year's Eve and the thought of not starting the next year of their lives together was making her want to crawl up into a ball.

She couldn't ask him to stay with her. It would be selfish and needy and throughout this entire relationship he had been the one to give to her. She wanted to give something back to him, but she didn't know how. How to show him that she loved him. Words just weren't enough anymore.

"I'm glad you conducted the interview. I wouldn't have thought to ask half of those questions. Thank you for doing that," she said awkwardly, when she knew there were a thousand other words that she should be saying.

"Stop thanking me." He dropped the shoes, grabbed her shoulders and pushed her down on the bed, his heavy body covering hers. It felt so good, having his hard, warm weight on top of her. She closed her eyes as he kissed down the side of her neck. She was going to miss this, too. The security of his arms. The instant arousal she felt whenever he touched her. "I didn't do anything special…"

"You did. I'm going to miss you."

"It's just three days. You'll be on a flight back to New York and I'll come get you from the airport." He kissed her cheek. "I'll take you out for a nice dinner and then back to the apartment and I'll strip every inch of clothing you have off of you. You won't be able to go to work the next day because I won't let you out of that bed."

"Asa." Her voice came out choked as tears escaped her eyes. "Because I can't go back to New York."

He was quiet for an incredibly long time.

"I knew you were going to tell me that." He rolled off her and lay beside her on the bed, his arm over his eyes.

"What do you mean you knew?"

"I knew. I was just hoping you weren't going to say that."

"I know we hired a nurse and that there's help here for them, but I just can't leave my mother and grandmother right now. Maybe in a few weeks or a month. I don't want to lose you."

"I don't think you'll ever be able to leave them. I don't want this to end, either. I want to be selfish. I want to just let you come back and pretend I don't know that your heart isn't completely here. But I can't do that. Because in my heart, I'll know you're there for the wrong reason and it will make me feel like hell."

"Damn it, Asa. Don't do this. Don't end this. I would be happy with you anywhere on the planet. I *will* be happy for you. But I just can't go now."

"You can't start a new life unless you really know what kind of life you want. Maybe you're not ready to be in a relationship yet. This was too soon for you. You told me you had all these plans. You were going to finish your doctorate and become a professor. You said you gave that up for Brent. He's out of the picture. What's stopping you now?"

She froze. That was a damn good question. She could blame the move, and the new job, and life getting in the way, but those were all just excuses. She'd run away from heartbreak, but she hadn't run toward her goals in the process. "I don't know."

"I need you to be sure."

She did know what she wanted out of life. She wanted him and marriage and babies. She wanted to live her life right here on this island and be surrounded by her family. But could she ask that of him? After six weeks? Especially since she knew how much he loved New York, how good he was at his job. She saw him with her grandmother and mother and speaking to the doctors in the hospital, and she knew that the FDNY would lose one of the best rescue paramedics they had ever had. Asa meant healer and being a healer was his calling. She couldn't ask him to give that up for her, because just like she didn't want her to resent him, she couldn't bear the thought of Asa resenting her.

"Asa..." She reached for his hand, her heart breaking. She knew this was ending for the right reasons but it felt so wrong, so incredibly wrong. Her days had been a little brighter these past few weeks knowing that he was in them.

"Hallie," he whispered. "Don't look at me like that."

"Like what? Like the love of my life isn't walking away from me?" She felt the first tear slip from her eye and she realized she was crying over him. She hadn't cried for Brent. She had been angry and hurt and shocked, but this was a different kind of devastation. She had been so close to touching the kind of happiness that she only thought was possible in fiction.

Asa took in a deep sharp breath and pressed his head to hers. "You've got to come back to New York. All of your things are there. You'll see me again. You have to see me again."

She nodded, but she knew she really didn't have to go back if she didn't want to. She wasn't taking her furniture. She had all her important things with her. It would just be some clothes and things she could replace. The only reason she would go back was to see him. Saying goodbye to him twice would be impossible. She couldn't do it again. She wasn't ready to do it now.

She sat up and slipped her dress off over her head. "Make love to me. Please. One more time before you go."

He reached for her and nodded just before he removed the rest of her clothing. "One time will never be enough with you."

Chapter 20

Asa had said his goodbyes to most of his family that morning when he went to visit them at Carlos and Virginia's house. He had said goodbye to Hallie at his rental house even though he thought he would have more time with her. He had anticipated that she would go with him to the ferry and kiss him goodbye, but she didn't want to. She just gave him a brief, tight hug before she turned away. She wouldn't look him in the eye one last time before she walked out the door for good. She was hurting. Tremendously so, and he felt like scum because of it.

"Looks like it's really going to come down," Virginia said, looking out the window as they drove toward the ferry. "It's supposed to storm tonight. It's going to ruin a lot of New Year's plans. Hopefully your flight will get out on time."

"Yeah," he said only half listening to her.

Just Virginia had come to take him to the ferry. They hadn't had any time alone during his two weeks there and this seemed like it would be their only opportunity. He knew he should be focusing on her, but he couldn't get the look on Hallie's face out of his mind and as he drove further and further away from her, he felt more and more like he was leaving half his heart behind.

Virginia pulled to a stop in front of the ferry terminal and rested her hand on her growing belly. Something inside of him pulled agonizingly as he watched her do that simple action. She was going to have a baby, be a mother, start a new big chapter in her life and he wouldn't be there. He would be in New York, alone. Completely alone, doing a job he no longer loved. His parents wouldn't even be nearby.

Why was he going back? He had been so focused on what Hallie wanted and how she could be happy that he'd barely thought about what he really wanted out of life.

Hallie loved him. She said so. She had called him the love of her life. A person didn't just say that. Hallie wouldn't just say that. She must have meant it.

"Asa, I don't want to pry into your private life, but what happened between you and Hallie?"

"What? Why are you asking?"

"She's not here and you look like you want to die."

"We broke up."

"What do you mean you broke up?"

He shook his head. "I didn't want her to sacrifice her happiness by staying in New York just for me. I didn't want her to end up resenting me."

"You broke up with her now, so she wouldn't break up with you later? How does that make sense at all?"

"I don't know."

"A person can find happiness anywhere if they choose to. Something brought you two together. Something powerful keeps throwing you together. Out of all the paramedics in the world, you were the one to respond to that call. Out of all the places in the world for you two to spend the holidays, you both ended up here where your families are.

She doesn't have to go back to New York to be with you, because she already went there to find you."

Asa took in a deep, sharp breath, his head spinning from his sister's impassioned speech.

"You can't let her go. You love her."

Virginia stroked her belly and looked down at her feet. "I've never seen you this happy before. If you let her go, I'm afraid you won't be this happy again."

She was right. He knew deep in his soul that he wouldn't find someone like her again. He could come here. His family was here now. He could work here. Carlos had given him a huge opportunity and if he didn't like it, he could always find something else to do. But he wouldn't find another Hallie. "I think I just made the biggest mistake of my life."

A brilliant flash of purplish lightning followed by an enormous crack of thunder surrounded him—it felt like the entire island shook. And then Asa's phone went off. An alert from the airlines telling him that his flight had been canceled due to weather.

Fate.

Destiny.

Forever.

Virginia and Asa stared at each other, their eyes wide, their minds thinking the same exact thing. "Turn this car around and take me back to your house," he said to his sister. "If I'm going to make a gesture, it needs to be a big one."

It was late by the time he had put together everything for Hallie and so when he showed up at her parents' home that night he was nervous and excited. He was also soaking wet because the skies had decided to open up and give him a real taste of how powerful an island storm could be. It took a few minutes of knocking before someone answered the door. He knew that it must have been hard to hear over the howling wind and the thunder roaring around him. But Derek answered the door, clearly surprised to see him standing there.

"What are you doing out in this storm?" He pulled Asa inside. "Are you insane? The wind is supposed to get stronger."

"I came to see Hallie. I need to ask her something. I need to ask you all something."

"You want to marry her, I suppose?" Clara asked from the overstuffed easy chair in the living room.

"Yes. I've come to ask for your permission."

"Some might say that's terribly old-fashioned and it's not up to the parents to have a say in who their daughter wants to spend the rest of her life with."

"Maybe. I'm going to ask her anyway, with or without your permission. But I was hoping you would give it."

"She gives her permission." Nanny appeared from the back of the house, all bundled up in a bathrobe.

"Mother!"

"You like the boy. Stop giving him a hard time."

"I like him, too," Derek said. "Especially after how he stepped up and helped this week."

"You all never let me have any fun," Clara sighed. "You have my blessing. I've already told you as much. I just wanted to give you a hard time like my husband would have. She's our only child. I also wanted to make you sweat it out because she came back here very upset and refused to talk to any of us about it."

"Where is she?" he asked, his heart beating faster. "I think I can fix that."

"That's the thing," Derek said with a slight worried look on his face. "She's not here. She called me to come over and then she took off. We don't know where she is."

* * *

The teakettle on the small ancient stove in the boathouse sounded and Hallie tore her eyes away from the storm that was lighting up the ocean to attend to it. She had come here to think. It was the only place on the island where she could be alone with her thoughts and yet she didn't have very many thoughts tonight. Just one. And it was how to make Asa believe that her life wouldn't be complete without him.

Asa was gone and she was faced with the prospect of spending every day without him, sleeping without his strong arms around her, with not having him there to lean on. She was no longer sure she could be happy here. And he would be without her. He would come home to a cold, dark apartment. There would be no one there to speak to about his day. No one to share his meals with. No one to love him. He loved so hard, and so deeply that he deserved to get the same in return. No one would love him like she would. It would be impossible.

She retrieved the sugar from the cabinet and stirred the tea in her mug for far too long. She heard pounding, figured it was the wind beating against the little boathouse and ignored it. But when she turned around she saw a man standing at the door. She screamed, but then she recognized who it was.

Through the wind and the hammering rain she recognized the missing piece of her heart. She rushed to open the door and the force of the wind blew it back, causing it to slam against the wall. Asa stepped inside, soaked to the bone, grim determination on his face.

"What are you doing here?" she yelled out to him but she couldn't even hear her own words over the force of the storm. She just pulled him further into the house and together they pushed the door shut.

"Why the hell are you in the most dangerous place on the island during one of the worst storms of the year? You could have been killed. This little house could have blown away!"

"I'm fine. *You* could have been killed! You drove in this. And then you walked up to the house. You could have been blown into the ocean."

"I came to find you. Not even twenty-mile-per-hour winds are going to stop me."

"What are you doing here?" She turned away, rushing to the closet to get out a towel and a blanket for him. "You were supposed to be on a plane."

"No, I'm not."

He was dripping wet, water running off his face, his clothes plastered to his body. Her heart was in her throat. Anything could have happened to him. And if something did… She wasn't sure she would be able to recover. She grabbed his shoulders and began peeling off his wet clothing, the rain slicker he was wearing that didn't seem to help one bit and the navy blue shirt that was plastered to his chest.

When she unbuttoned his pants, he grabbed her arms and kissed her till she was breathless and she couldn't make her mind work. She was so focused on the fact that he was there that she forgot to think about the reason he was there.

She grabbed the towel and dragged it across his chest when he released her. "Get out of those pants. I know you can't catch a cold from being cold, but it can't be good for you to be in sopping wet clothing."

"You've been crying." He touched her face.

"Of course I've been crying. You left."

"I couldn't go."

"Because of this storm?"

"I couldn't go home because you weren't going to be there. My home is not in New York. My home is wherever you are."

"My home is where *you* are," she told him. "I was coming back to New York. I was going to pound down your door and make you listen to me tell you why I loved you until you believed it. I—"

"Hush." He stepped away from her and reached into his jacket, pulling out a soggy packet of papers. "I need to tell you something. I bought a house."

"What?"

"I bought the rental house we stayed in. You said you liked it so I bought it. Virginia's going to decorate it. She said she could get started right away."

She shook her head. "That house must have cost a fortune. I was just talking when I said I could live there. I didn't mean for you to buy it."

"It's perfect for us. I was thinking we could turn the third bedroom into an office for you."

She was having a hard time processing what he was saying, his presence there after she was sure he had gone. "What exactly are you trying to tell me?"

"That I'm an idiot. A huge one. I just wanted you to be sure of what you wanted, sure of us, that it almost caused me to lose you. I never thought about the life I wanted."

"What kind of life do you want?"

"The kind where I spend the rest of it with you. Here on this island."

"But what about your job? Your apartment? You love New York. I would never dream of asking you to give it up for me."

"Why not? You were willing to give up this place for me. Your soul is here. The memories of your father, the people you love the most. I can give New York up for you. But I can't give you up."

"I want you to be happy."

"I won't be without you."

Her heart was beating so hard that she was having a hard time breathing. "What does this mean for you?"

"I quit my job."

"But you're so good at it."

"I'm not going back. I'm done with seeing people in pain and at their worst. I want to see people at their best. That job brought me to you and I think it was fate that brought us together. I don't need to do it anymore, because I already got the best thing that ever came from that job."

"Where will you work? I know you. I know you like to stay active."

He nodded. "Carlos is starting a foundation for student athletes who come from areas with limited access to resources. He wants me to run the day-to-day operations here on the island."

Hallie eased herself into the nearest chair. "That's a big deal, Asa. Are you sure it's what you want? You've never had a desk job before."

"It won't be just a desk job. I'll get to work with kids and one of my best friends to do something good."

"It sounds like a good opportunity. I know you'll do a lot of good."

"He's opening up a camp here in the summer for them and they are going to focus on the arts and academics as well as sports. He said he could use someone to oversee the education side. I recommended you."

"What?"

"It doesn't have to be forever, just until you get a job as a professor. Most of the work will be in the summer when you're not in class or working on your dissertation."

"My dissertation..." This was all getting to be so much. "I'm going back to school?"

"If you want to. That's what I want for you. I want my wife to have everything she's dreamed of having. I want to raise our family here. I want you to wake up every morning knowing how much I love you."

She had been waiting to hear those words from him and it was better than she imagined, much sweeter. It made her heart squeeze. "Asa..." The tears rolled down her face. "I love you, too."

"I know." He went down on his knee before her and slipped a ring out of his pocket. "And that's why I'm asking you to marry me. My life is no good without you."

She nodded. She couldn't speak. She just couldn't get out the words.

He smiled at her, pulled her into her arms and kissed her for what seemed like hours. She broke the kiss and just held on to him for a while, savoring the knowledge that she was going to spend the rest of her life with a man who was perfect for her, who was her destiny.

"Look." Asa pointed to the clock on the wall behind her. "It's midnight. Happy New Year. Our Christmas break is officially over."

"Yes, but it's the start of a great new year."

"The best year," he said as he kissed her.

"The best year," Hallie agreed as she kissed him back.

She was never one to believe in happily-ever-afters but with Asa at her side she was sure she was going to get one.

* * * * *

Earn
FREE
REWARDS
Join
Today!
HarlequinMyRewards.com